Sabre Tooth

D1610884

R. M. CARTMEL

A Sequel to Oliver Richbell's Novella

GLORIANA

Inspired by the Motion Picture

The Day of the Jackal

ISBN: 978-1-910040-40-9

SABRE TOOTH

She had long golden hair that hung down in waves, over the back of the chaise longue, framing her tanned, heart shaped face. Her eyes were bright green with brown flecks in the irises while her mouth wore an ironic smile. At her other extremity were two long slender legs, encased in silk, the outer one of which dangled off the couch onto the floor. The other hung over the back of the chaise at an angle of ninety degrees at the knee. Both legs disappeared into a shortish skirt that had risen up to just below where decency might become questionable. Her blouse appeared to have been unbuttoned, rather than pulled apart.

'Is that what akimbo means?' asked the uniformed sergeant standing by; 'What a waste.'

The DI flicked his glance down to her bare abdomen just in case the sergeant had seen something he hadn't, but no there was nothing remarkable there that wasn't already noted. Their eyes couldn't help focusing on the long decorated ivory shaft that stood erect between her breasts. From her expression, she must have died before she realised what was happening. There was little blood to be seen round the wound.

'Doesn't look like she was expecting it,' said the sergeant after a further pause.

D.I. Gray looked at her hands, and wrists. Apart from a small watch on her left wrist there was no jewellery to be seen and there were no tan lines on her fingers to suggest that a ring had been removed.

'Do we know who she was guv?' asked the sergeant, trying to get some response out of the Detective Inspector.

'Oh yes.' He replied, 'That's Sierra Nicholls.'

'Rings a bell,' he replied, 'just not a very loud one. Remind me who she was?'

'Freelance journalist, appearing on an increasing number of TV shows. Was apparently quite a fan of Brexit.'

'You think this is politically motivated guv?'

'Could be anything at this stage. Any signs of robbery?' he asked rather more loudly to the other uniforms in the room.

'Nothing obvious,' came back a hubbub of noncommittal voices.

The photographer took her pictures and the forensic team appeared watching DI Gray, who watched them in return. There really wasn't anything in the room to suggest untoward happenings, apart from the presence of the dead woman in the middle of it. 'Sarge,' he said. 'Can you package up her laptop for forensics to check out? I want to look at what she was writing and there may be prints on it.'

'There may be prints everywhere, guv,' he replied. 'If he was someone she knew and presumably liked, it's unlikely he was wearing gloves, especially as he was undressing her.'

'Do we know she wasn't already half-undressed before he came in and knifed her?' replied the DI. 'We need to establish a moment-by-moment timeline. Don't we doc?' Dr Lawrence, a dry grey haired woman, who hadn't apparently taken any effort to help her appearance, smiled at him grimly. 'Can you start on her tonight?' he asked.

'I think so,' she replied, 'The sooner we put the bastard who did this behind bars, the more comfortably I'll sleep at night.'

'Any idea how long ago this happened?' he asked.

'Not long, she's still warm, and there's no sign of rigor mortis yet. I'll let you know when I get her back to the lab, which will be about ten minutes after you release the body from here.'

'Take her away Doc,' he replied. And the dance of the forensic team began in earnest. The body bag on a gurney appeared from nowhere. It had always amazed him how unwieldy a corpse was to manhandle, however lightly constructed it was. The limbs, arranged admittedly chaotically to start with, became suddenly floppier. They were everywhere, inconvenient when the technicians tried to move the body and put it on top of the bag on the gurney. The bag was then wrapped round her and zipped shut. The gurney was wheeled out and Sierra Nicholls was no longer in her flat.

§§§§

'No prints on the laptop apart from her own,' said the Sergeant, but she had a very complicated password system, which has us stumped at the moment.

'Anybody spare at IT to have a look at it?'

'Ahmed's already had a go, but he's spotted a logic bomb in there.'

'A logic bomb?'

'It will wipe the hard drive, if he goes any further.'

'Can he take a copy of that drive, and work on that? That way if he does lose all the data we've at least not lost the information.'

'I'll ask him. It is of course possible that copying the drive will set off the logic bomb.'

'Tell him to do his best. What was she being so protective over? She was a journalist for Chrissakes, the whole point of what she was writing was that it would be read by the general public.'

'It might well be a time sensitive article guv. You know, somebody gave her a scoop provided it was only to be printed on such and such a day, as decreed by the "scoopee". And people who break those sort of agreements don't often get awarded scoops again further down the line.'

'You like that word "Scoop", don't you? Well let's hope we can get to read it then,' the DI went to make himself a cup of coffee to help him think.

§§§§

Dr Lawrence was looking thoughtfully at her work when the DI appeared. 'Cause of death doc?' he asked, 'the stab-wound?'

'Oh yes,' she replied. 'Cardiac tamponade, caused when the dagger went into and through the right ventricle. She bled into the pericardium instantly. The weapon was a very long thin dress dagger, but what is really interesting is that it passed through the sternum into the heart, and not between the ribs. It would have required a great deal of force to do that. The sternum is sensitive, and therefore it must have been a single movement for it to have happened that way. The dagger was certainly very sharp, but to have passed straight through the sternum required a great deal of force behind it. A great deal.' She added the last slowly and thoughtfully.

'So the killer was big,' he said.

'Or very strong.'

'Was it a chemically assisted kill?' he asked. 'You know, had she been sedated first? Alcohol, benzos?'

'Those tests are under way as we speak. There was some alcohol in her system, but looking at the general state of her liver, I suspect that was not a particularly uncommon occurrence.'

'Bad cirrhosis?' he asked.

'Oh no, nothing like that, just a little fatty degradation, but when you look at the general amount of body fat as a whole, it was probably due to a little too much than was good for her, if you know what I mean.'

'Had she been sexually assaulted?'

'No evidence of any recent penetration.' The old woman paused for a moment, cleared her throat, and then continued, 'although the presence of a reasonable amount of vaginal fluid suggests that she was anticipating congress in the imminent future, and was quite looking forward to it.'

'So you're suggesting she knew her killer?'

'Not necessarily, just that she would have found sexual congress with him or her acceptable.'

'What aren't you telling me Doc? Is there evidence that she was a woman of questionable morals?'

'Not at all, there was no evidence during the autopsy of what her orientation was, nor what her morals were. All we know was that she had consumed alcohol on a regular basis, and has had sex in the past. The presence of a contraceptive implant in her left arm suggests that she was willing to take responsibility for her own contraceptive needs. She also had a scar in the upper right arm, where a previous implant had been removed, suggesting that she found a contraceptive implant an acceptable form of contraception. Generally it's recommended that an implant is changed every three years, if you want to count on it remaining effective. Nobody knows what happens if you leave an implant in after the three years are up, so old implants are always removed. It's possible, that if they're left in for over a decade, they might scar in so completely, that they would be impossible to remove. That might prove a problem if the woman would subsequently wish to become pregnant. Bearing in mind that this was at the very least her second implant, suggests that she had been sexually active with a male of the species somewhere along the line, though it says nothing about her current orientation.'

'Are you suggesting that people can be cured of homosexuality Doc?'

'Heaven forefend! However, some people do change their minds from time to time! That's why we have General Elections every now and then.'

The pathologist paused for a moment, and then showed him the weapon. He recognised the shiny off-white haft. 'What do you think of this?' she asked.

The blade was very narrow and came to a very sharp point. The ivory handle had a pewter pommel at the top end, and below the ivory grip was a cross guard, which also looked like it was made from pewter. Both the pommel and the cross guard were decorated by a swastika, rotated at 45 degrees from the horizontal. 'Is that a Nazi dagger?' he asked.

'It appears so. Probably it was an officer's dress dagger, which went with his uniform on formal occasions. It was probably never intended to be used as a weapon as such. It would be very interesting to analyse the steel, and what it was actually made of. It passed through the Sternum, through the right ventricle and embedded itself in the vertebral cartilage behind the heart. It would have taken a great deal of force to get it that far in one movement. She died instantly. However once it was in, there was no way it was coming out again. It required dissecting out at autopsy.'

'Could she have committed suicide with it?'

'Yes, but not have ended up in the position she was in, afterwards.'

'How do you mean?'

'Well she could have fallen on it, but she was found supine on the chaise longue, and I don't think she had the strength in her arms to have inflicted that wound. So if she had killed herself, someone came along and arranged her body in the way that you found her. I did check, but there were no fingerprints at all on the haft, not even hers.'

DI Gray felt something tingling in his pocket. He pulled out his phone. He apologised, 'I'm sorry, I must take this,' and walked to the door.

'Hello guv, DI Gray here.'

'Hello Gray,' came the gruff voice of the Super, 'You busy?'

'I'm in the mortuary going over a post mortem with the pathologist.'

'I need you now,' came back down the line. 'I'll send McGregor over to take over from you there.'

'But it's important to the case I'm working on.'

'So McGregor can take over the case too. What is this case?'

'Sierra Nicholls.'

'Why, what's she done now? I assume you mean the posh news hack with the nice voice who's all over the news programmes at the moment as a sort of vox pop who sounds like she knows what she's talking about.'

'Sounds like her.'

'So, I'll ask again, what has she done now?'

'Currently she's lying on the pathologists table having undergone a post mortem exam.'

'She's dead? There's a facer. McGregor will enjoy that one.'

'But sir, may I state once again, it's my case.'

'Not anymore, you're needed with me, Secretary of State's orders.'

'The Secretary of State?'

'Asked for you by name.'

'What's it all about?'

'I've no idea. They asked for you by name, and they're sending a car for you now. So I'm afraid you're going to have to tell Dr Lawrence she'll have to wait until McGregor can get to her, and then do her briefing all over again.'

'She's not going to be happy.'

'Can you ever remember a time when Dr Lawrence could be described, as happy? Now get your backside back to the station PDQ. I want you to be here and waiting when your transport arrives.'

'Sir,' Gray said and walked back into the post mortem room. He explained the situation to the pathologist as best he could, bearing in mind he hadn't the faintest idea what was going on. Dr McGregor gave him an expression like a bulldog chewing a wasp, and asked him if he was about to be suspended for something disciplinary. He replied that he didn't think so. He left his notes behind for McGregor to catch up on the case from, and left him his mobile number, in case he hadn't got it. He bade the pathologist farewell, and walked out into the English drizzle on his way back to the police station.

§§§§

There was a large black Jag parked outside the front steps of the police station. Gray walked through the front door just in time to hear the desk sergeant say, 'And here he is now. Talk about good timing or what!'

'What's this?' Gray asked.

'Your car sir,' said the Sergeant, 'to take you to Scotland Yard.'

He looked at the driver, scowled and asked for ID. The driver produced a pass. It was all a bit pointless really; there was no way he could actually tell if the face behind that COVID mask was the same face on the pass in front of him, but niceties still had to be observed in these troubled times. At least the driver had an official pass. 'Do I need to nip home and pack a bag, or are you bringing me back this evening?' Gray asked.

'I've only been booked for the next half hour,' replied the driver, 'but my instructions were quite definite, "now", and "no shilly-shallying", were both words I was told.'

'Let's go. Sarge, time me out and note my time of departure, and note this conversation. If I have to come back in a taxi, I'll be expecting the TVP to pick up the tab.'

'TVP?' asked the driver.

'Thames Valley Police,' he replied, 'my paymasters. Lead on.' He grabbed a mask from the box on the desk and followed the driver out. He was contemplating on parking himself in the back seat, but his hand automatically went to the left front door, and he climbed in and pulled the seat belt around him. If the driver objected to his sitting in the front, he showed no signs of it.

'So, what do they want me for in Scotland Yard?' he asked the driver as they pulled out into traffic.

'I've no idea, sir, I'm only a driver. You don't think they actually tell me things do you?'

Gray thought it was going to be a very dull journey. He just hoped the driver wasn't going to talk about football to disguise the embarrassment of travelling in silence.

§§§§

'Follow me,' said the driver as he stopped by the side door of a building that didn't look like any form of Scotland Yard that he remembered. Was he being abducted? He was about to say to the driver sitting on his right words to the effect of 'what's going on?' when he realised that the driver had already got out of the car, and was opening the side door in front of them. 'Come on,' he tossed over his shoulder at Gray. Through the door he found himself in a typical police station anteroom, with a rather constipated looking uniformed police sergeant, sitting behind a bar, talking animatedly on the phone. Watts interrupted the Sergeant's flow with, 'Inspector Gray, as required.'

The sergeant looked even more uncomfortable, and whimpered, 'Sir! Please follow me.' He put the phone back on its cradle without explaining himself to the unfortunate person on the other end of the line. He swung himself round the counter, and scuttled off down a corridor to his left, deep into the bowels of the building. Every now and then he looked over his shoulder to reassure himself that Gray was still following him, and relieved that he still was, he bustled on. Gray could imagine him rubbing one ear and muttering, 'Oh my fur and whiskers,' to himself. The corridor finally ended up in a large atrium, with natural light coming in from a high, vee shaped glass ceiling. There were various chairs with coffee tables near them, on which magazines were laid out. The magazines were still fanned so obviously nobody had actually waited in the atrium that day.

Across the atrium was a large double door, which would have completely blocked the corridor they had just walked down. The sergeant walked straight towards it, and as he reached it, he turned round and faced Gray, 'Here we are;' he said, 'ready?'

'For what?' Gray replied icily. It felt like he had been kidnapped in darkest Buckinghamshire, and driven all the way into London without anybody explaining anything to him on the way.

'They'll explain,' said the sergeant, and throwing the door open, he announced to the room, in a far more stentorian voice than he had shown Gray that he was capable of, 'Inspector Gray.' He then stood aside and left Gray facing a room with a large oblong table in the middle of it. On the walls hung portraits of people Gray did not recognise, but from the way they were painted, they were probably important people at the time the pictures were completed. Around the table designed to seat a considerably larger number of people than were actually there, were various men and women sitting a regulation two metres apart all wearing an expression suggesting that they too would like their portraits to be up on that wall. He even recognised a couple of them. The woman sitting at the far end of the table was the Home Secretary.

Directly in front of him there was an empty chair, and then the other person he recognised, the Commissioner of the Metropolitan Police, sitting to the left of the Home Secretary, greeted him, and asked him to remove his mask so that he could be formally identified. He did so. The Commissioner told the room that this was indeed DI Gray of the Thames Valley Police, and invited him to sit in the empty chair. Gray did so.

'I expect you're wondering what you're doing here,' said the Commissioner.

'Just a bit,' replied Gray, 'an hour ago I was in the middle of a case.'

'Yes quite,' said the Commissioner, not apparently showing the slightest interest. 'You've been brought here because we need your skills,' she continued. The inspector had never been that close to the Commissioner before, and that close up she looked a lot more lined and grey than she did from a distance. He developed an increased respect for the television make-up departments at that moment.

Gray said nothing. No doubt they would explain which skills they were interested in. It was probably not his ability at table tennis that had caught their fancy.

At this dramatic juncture, the Home Secretary took up the story, 'I need a good detective, who is not a member of the Metropolitan Police, but part of a different constabulary, and your name came up. I need a detective we can trust, and at the same time whose face is not known in London. We think that man is you.'

'And you want me to do what?' he asked.

'You remember that attempt on the Prime Minister's life a couple of months ago, in 10 Downing Street.'

'I thought that was a successful terrorist attempt to blow up a Saudi Trade delegation. That was how it was reported in the paper anyway, and that the perpetrators are, shall we say, no longer needing to breathe.'

'We think that the Trade Delegation was collateral damage, and that the attempt was aimed at the Prime Minister himself. We think that there was a much wider cabal than just General Llewellyn-Jones, and Sebastian Pennington, and that there will be a further attempt on the PM's life.'

'But an attempt at that time was surely to prevent Brexit happening, and now it's happened and Britain has left the EU, without needing any vestige of a deal to still be on the table, assassinating the PM now just seems to be a pointless, rather spiteful gesture of revenge.'

"Hmm,' muttered the Home Secretary, 'Philip Nicholson, who is now considered to be the *éminence grise* of the whole plot …'

'Philip Nicholson?' Gray interrupted.

'He used to be the Master of the Royal Household and is, I understand, hiding away somewhere in Europe; exactly where isn't known on this side of the channel, but after the way that the UK left the EU, we don't appear to be on speaking terms with any of the police forces of the individual Countries of Europe. We did ask the head office of Europol for their help in tracking him down, and we were told to go away and stop bothering them as they had more important things to do for more interesting countries than us. As we're no longer a member of their exclusive club, they went on to explain, and as that situation was entirely of our own making, they could see absolutely no reason to help us. Moreover they were under strict orders from the powers that be that none whatsoever will be available until we've paid up the £39bn divorce settlement they claim we still owe. Their off the cuff view is that the only country who might have any reason to get involved anyway in a manhunt for Philip Nicholson might be the Saudis. It is apparently the view of whichever country in which Nicholson is hiding, that the crime happened in Britain, and therefore it's a British problem and not theirs, and they're not getting involved.'

'So at least you know which country he's hiding in?' Gray said hopefully.

'No, it just seems to be a collective view they've all taken.'

'So if one of their leaders got assassinated on British soil, they wouldn't expect us to help them?'

'I think the chances of any European leader setting foot on English soil is not very great at this moment in time,' the Home Secretary replied dryly.

'So what do you want me to do?'

'We want you to stop this next assassination attempt, and round up the rest of the cabal who is attempting to carry it out.'

'So what other information do you have?'

'That it's going to happen soon.'

'How soon?'

'We don't know.'

'Where?'

'We don't know.' The Home Secretary's expression

became increasingly pained, as she confessed to ever increasing levels of ignorance.

'You mean all you know is that someone's going to try to kill the PM and you want me to stop them?'

'That's the long and short of it.'

'Well on the assumption that the Prime Minister will be at the same location as he will be when he's to be assassinated, I will need a complete list of what he will be doing for the weeks to come, down to lunch and toilet breaks.'

'I'm not sure he will allow that.' She was positively sweating with anxiety by this point.

'Everything he doesn't allow increases his risk. If I can't predict where he's going to be, then I can't protect him. I presume he wants someone to stop him being killed? And another thing, his habit of outside women, has to stop right now.'

'Outside women?'

'You can't please your wife and your outside woman too.' Gray sounded almost lyrical for a moment as he quoted from the old blues standard by Blind Joe Reynolds. As this cultural aside drew no response whatever from the floor, he continued, 'What resources have I got?'

'Anything you like.'

'Money?'

'Within reason.'

'I would like a small team to work with. I want people I know, so that I understand how their brains work.'

'You've got it. Are they all police?'

'They're all members of *a* force, yes.'

'Commissioner, take their details, and get them seconded to me or Inspector Gray immediately.'

'Where will I be working from?'

'We'll give you a safe house with attached office space.'

'Oh, and Inspector, we require the utmost discretion. This conversation has never happened once you have left this room.'

'I assume that blanket ban excludes the members of my team. If it doesn't, I can't work under those limitations.'

'Of course,' snapped the Police Commissioner, 'Do you think we're idiots?'

Gray didn't bother to reply, but looked round the other people sitting round the table. On Gray's right they wore uniform, the Commissioner, an Army General, and an Air Marshal, all wearing a lot of scrambled egg on their uniforms. Interesting, he thought, that the Navy wasn't represented. On his left they all appeared to be civilians. They were certainly all in mufti. They were all approaching the age when they were turning grey apart from the Home Secretary herself. The Inspector wondered whether her hair colour was chemically assisted. Maybe she could hear his thoughts, as she puckered her mouth and said, 'I think that's all we need from you at the moment Inspector. You will liaise at a very minimum daily with the Commissioner here, and you will notify him immediately you have selected your team. You have twenty four hours to put your team in place.'

'Yes ma'am,' he said.

'You may go,' she told him, in a voice that couldn't have been more dismissive if it had been accompanied by a flap of the back of her hand.

Gently amused, Gray got up and left the room. The commissioner herself joined him in the atrium a moment later. She was rummaging in her pocket as she came out through the double door. She gave him a bit of paper with an address on it. 'When you get to the front, ask the guy on the desk for Sergeant Watts and a car. Watts knows this address, and a piece of free advice; you'd do a lot worse if you were to pick him as a member of your team. Firstly, he will know where your base of operations is. On top of that he knows more about the streets of London than any black cab driver I have met. He's also very skilled at tactical driving.'

'Tactical driving, guv?'

'He is very skilled at tailing someone without being spotted, and also at spotting a tail that's following him, and losing it. If he's your driver, I won't lay claim to him while this operation is on-going.'

Gray looked at the elderly woman for a moment, and smiled. He got the impression that he had just received a very handy gift. 'Thank you guv,' he replied.

'There's an Inspector Anson, who will be round to your flat shortly. He's a very bright young man, and very capable of thinking outside the box. May I recommend you make good use of his skills.'

'Yes ma'am, Anson. Got it.'

'One other thing,' said the Commissioner, pulling an iPhone out of her pocket. 'My number's programmed into this under the name, "Aunt Muriel."'

'Is that your name?'

'I'll leave you to work that out for yourself. Get this sorted out well, and your personal pass mark at your next promotion exam will be five per cent'

'And if I don't?'

'Probably closer to a hundred and five! Best of luck Inspector Gray.' And exchanging a wry smile, she walked back through the double doors.

§§§§

Gray wandered down the corridor and approached the sergeant at the desk, who looked as if he had managed to find time to empty his bowel since they last met.

'Yes guv?' he asked.

'I was told you would know where a Sergeant Watts might be,' he replied.

The sergeant nodded at a weather beaten face atop a large body in a rather elderly pullover with leather patches on both elbows and a pair of jeans that had also seen better days. The man wandered over to the desk, 'I'm Watts,' he said.

'I'm pleased to meet you,' Gray replied. 'I gather you have a lift for me.'

'Follow me,' said Watts. 'Oh by the way,' said Watts, 'We're both in the same official bubble now, so we don't need to wear PPE in each other's presence.' They walked back down the corridor, which Gray had been walking up and down all morning. But when they had got no more than half way to the atrium, Watts came close to a door that to his surprise Gray realised he hadn't noticed during either journey. Watts pushed at the door, and it opened onto a stairwell leading downwards into a basement garage. Watts pulled a key out of his pocket, and pressed a button on it. The lights of a slightly grubby silver-grey Vauxhall Vectra flashed at them. 'Our ride,' he said.

Gray climbed into the front passenger seat and Watts grinned at him. He pulled the car out of its bay, and just for a moment, he floored the accelerator. The engine growled like no Vauxhall he had ever heard before, and the car leapt forward. Watts kept smiling and removed his foot from the pedal.

'What the hell has this car got under the bonnet?'

Gray asked.

'A 6 litre Holden Commodore engine in case we need it. However if we caress it along quietly, no one will be any the wiser.'

'A police special?'

'The Met's got all sorts of interesting unmarked cars in its fleet.'

'I'm beginning to look forward to what this flat is going to look like,' said Gray. 'Am I going to be equally surprised?'

'Don't know; depends on what surprises you, I suppose.'

§§§§

The flat was in fact a semi-detached house within an Edwardian looking street. The road had two ends, and had parking restrictions. In front of the house, where presumably a lawn had once been, there was now a gravel park for three cars. There was also an attached garage to the side of the house. Around the pair of houses was a low privet hedge, which had been beautifully maintained. Watts reversed up to the garage doors such that you couldn't open them from within. He then got out of the car, and suggesting that Gray followed him, walked up to the front door. The inspector was interested to notice that the keys that opened the front door, a brass Chubb and then a Yale deadlock, were already on the car key ring. The house was a lot more modern inside than suggested by its Edwardian exterior and had obviously been recently refurbished. The kitchen had all the mod cons, and Gray was pleased to note that there was a state of the art coffee machine, and that someone had put two pint-cartons of fresh milk in the fridge. He looked at them closely, yes they were still in date, and so they weren't left over from the last time the safe house was occupied, however many months ago that was.

'Coffee?' he asked Watts.

'Why not,' Watts replied.

There was a sound of footsteps on the stairs and he was very surprised to see a girl walking down towards them. She looked strangely monochrome surrounded by the colour of the carpet and walls.

'And you are?' he asked brusquely.

'Polly Stokes,' she replied. 'I come with the house. You must be Inspector Gray.'

'And how do you know that?'

'Well, you're not Watts, so it stands to reason you must be Inspector Gray.'

'And so I ask again, why are you here?'

'I come with the house. I'm a sort of assistant, secretary, Girl Friday, etcetera. If you need anything done in the house, me or one of the other girls will do it.'

'One of the other girls?' It was becoming more surreal by the moment.

'Yes, there's three of us. At any one time, one of us will be on duty round the clock. The other two of us are all in the same bubble, and they're off duty in the house next door. That's how it works here; this house is the work house and next door is strictly off duty, and we do not talk work in there. If we want to talk work, we come back into this house. Got it?' Three of them, he thought, horrified at having three plain chubby Goths with black eyeliner and chains everywhere he looked.

'So where are you from?'

'We're all supplied by the Met,' she said drily.

'Do you make coffee?' he asked.

'Typical male,' she said, 'Walks through the door and immediately expects to be waited on.' She paused, and then continued, 'Yeah I can make coffee. Milk and sugar?'

'No sugar for me,' he replied, 'Don't know about Watts though.'

'I do,' she replied. 'He takes both.'

He looked at her askance, 'Are you two an item or something?'

'Me and Watts? You've got to be joking. That old bugger? Don't say that anywhere near my boyfriend, or he'll lamp you for that when we next meet.'

'You've got a boyfriend,' he asked hoping that he didn't sound so disbelieving to the unfortunate looking girl in front of him.

'Course I've got a boyfriend,' she replied testily, 'nothing wrong with me.'

'Well, don't go talking to him about what goes on in here. A bit of discretion is in order here.'

'You think I'd tell him we're trying to stop someone killing the PM? Are you nuts? He's a Remainer is my boyfriend. If he thought someone was going to off the PM, he'd buy him a pint. Now my dad on the other hand…'

'Go on,'

'Well my dad's not racist, 'cos he hates all forriners equally. As far as he's concerned Nig-Nogs start at Calais, and they don't get any *noggier* the further away from Calais you get. He'd approve of what you're doing Inspector Gray. I must introduce you to him, when I next get to see him.'

Gray shuddered, don't you dare, he thought.

'You're not going to talk about what we're doing to him either are you?' he said.

'Naa, just winding you up,' she said ignoring the coffee machine and pouring boiling water onto the grounds in the cafetière and stirring it.

'Here's yer coffee.'

Gray sat down at the table poured a drop of milk into the mug. He took a mouthful. 'You know something, that's really good,' he said with genuine surprise. She smiled an internal smile to herself. If it was going to become competitive with this Inspector Gray bloke, she'd won the opening round.

Gray took out the phone the Commissioner had given him, and tried one or two Europol numbers he carried in his head. The response was exactly as the Home Secretary had described it, insolently hostile. Okay so official channels weren't going to work. How about the Old Boy Network? For that, he needed his own phone. He went into his personal telephone directory, selected a number, and speed dialled it. It got an almost immediate response; 'Truchaud?' came out of the earpiece at him.

He replied in his best French, which actually wasn't that bad.

'*Le Loup Gris,*' Truchaud chuckled, once he had realised who was on the other end of the line, 'how are you, how are you doing now your country has decided that it's far too important to talk to anybody.'

A small amount of banter passed between both men as there often is when two old friends talk together for the first time in a while, after something momentous has happened to stop them getting together sooner.

Finally, the conversation got round to the nitty-gritty, Philip Nicholson. Truchaud didn't off hand know where he was hiding, no, but if it was really important to his old mate, the Gray Wolf, he would stir up the pot a little and see if anything rose to the surface. When did he need to know? Ah! As soon as possible eh? Gray had really got the monkey on his back had he? Well he would do his best, and he suggested that Gray called him back tomorrow.

§§§

Gray and Watts had hardly sat down when a thin, rather angular young man let himself in through the back door from the garden. 'Who are you? And how did you get in?' Gray asked.

'I'm Inspector Anson, and I've got a key,' came the reply. He acknowledged Watts and Polly by name. 'The Commissioner has asked me to see if I could be of assistance.'

'What do you have to offer?' asked Gray.

'Well, I'm a DI in the Met, so I've got local contacts, and I know how the city runs, if that's any help.'

Gray thought about it for a moment. Five years down the line, this young man would probably be offered the job he was doing at the moment. He was probably a little too young, that's all. If he was as bright as he looked, and had properly earned the respectful look Watts was giving him he might be very handy to have on board. 'Well, we're just settling in at the moment,' he replied. 'How can I get hold of you when I need you?'

'I've got a room next door, so if I'm not in here or next door, Polly and the others all know how to get in touch, so all you need to do is ask any of them.' Hmm, that also told him that there was a great deal more to the chubby young Goth than immediately met the eye.

§§§

Commander Truchaud of *la Police Nationale* based in the Quai d'Orfèvres, in Paris, sat on the customer side of his *Commandant Divisionaire*'s desk. The old chap was a genial lean and slipper'd pantaloon most of the time, but right at that moment his face was wearing a far more serious expression than it usually did.

'You mean you can't find him? Where did you lose him?' he said.

'He was last spotted on the other side of the Belgian border in a village called Adinkerque.'

'What was he doing there?'

'I understand he was drinking a cup of coffee. He was presumably waiting for someone.'

'Do we know who?'

'No, but if it was Adinkerque, the chances are that the person he was waiting for is English. Adinkerque is the first village over the border in Belgium, and most of its businesses there are tobacco and alcohol outlets, although some of the shops also sell excellent hand made Belgian chocolates and general bric-a-brac that might appeal to the lady left in the UK by the small town Englishman as domestic payment for the trip to Adinkerque. His view of the continent is that it's a source of 'duty-free' because the taxes on all those products are so much less in Belgium than they are in France or Britain. So the Brits come down the channel tunnel in cars or coaches and travel the hour it takes from Calais to Adinkerque, stock up on smokes and cheap wallop, and then it's back down to the tunnel again, to London in time for the evening meal. Before Brexit, it was a very good way of getting stuff back and forth into the street markets in and around London. The punters could then get their fags and booze cheaper from the street markets than it would cost them if they bought them at the local corner shop where those items would be properly taxed at the British rates. And the man in the van would easily cover his expenses, petrol and tunnel tickets out of the price he charged. The difference in the duty charged by the Belgian Government and their British counterparts on legal addictive substances really is that much. Did you know that Scotch Whisky is cheaper in Adinkerque than it is in the shop at its own distillery?'

'But even before Brexit happened, there was a certain maximum you could take back. Wasn't it described as enough for your own consumption?'

'I think that's how they described it, yes. However if you take back enough for your own consumption over the next three months on say Monday, and then you go back the following day and get another three month's supply, your stock quickly mounts up; especially if the driver's a teetotal non-smoker himself.'

'But since Brexit, they're back to the original duty free quantities being 200 fags and a litre of spirits. That surely won't make the business cost effective.'

'Er yes and no. Europol is aware that there are vans being serviced in the area, and the product is being built into the vans.'

'How do you mean?' the old man asked with a quizzical expression in his face.

'The way it works is that a man in a van goes down the tunnel, and goes to Adinkerque. That van, let's call it number one, goes into a workshop where they take the number plates off, and put them on an outwardly identical pre-prepared van, let's call that one number two, which has had cigarettes and booze built into it somewhere. The driver drives number two back to the

UK, having picked up his maximum Duty Free limit to avoid suspicion, plus some choccies and bric-a-brac, no doubt to sell on his market too. When he gets back to London, they put the number plates on yet another van, lets call that one number three, for the following day, while they take that day to unpack number two. Meanwhile, number one, the van he left behind in Belgium is being rebuilt with booty in Adinkerque.'

'Clever. Why don't the Belgian Police get involved?'

'There isn't a crime as such being committed on Belgian soil; all the Belgian tax on the tobacco and spirits *has* been paid up front, and gets to their Exchequer. So apart from the number plate sleight of hand, and as they're English number plates, *les Belges* aren't bothered. The first time a serious crime actually gets committed is when the consignment lands on English soil, when the stuff is sold on. It's the view of the Belgians that this is a problem for the English *douanes* and nothing to do with them. I've checked, there's no crime being committed against France in the short time the van is on French soil either. The product is not even exposed to the air while it's in France.'

'So why are you watching this at all, then?'

'Because we think it's also a way of keeping tabs on persons of interest to us; especially if they disappear over the border into Britain, and since Britain left the European Union, Europol has no influence in Britain.'

'You're telling me that there are no Europol agents in Britain at all now?'

'Of course there are, but they aren't working alongside Scotland Yard any longer, and they have no powers of arrest. So short of kidnapping and actual murder on the island, they have no executive power there. So most of the Europol people in Britain are surveillance experts, and most of them are English citizens. We think that that's how Mehdi Arraq got out of France. It looks like he was swapped in Belgium for someone else, and travelled back into Britain on this other fellow's British passport. Once Arraq was safely in the UK, he gave the passport back to the van driver, who drove back the next day to Adinkerque on his own, taking the papers back to bring the other fellow home, on his own documents.'

'And these famous surveillance experts aren't following Arraq?'

'They lost track of him somewhere in London,' Truchaud replied, embarrassed.

'Don't the British know this is going on?'

'Don't be silly; the British are only interested in controlling the migration from the EU. There's no real restriction on movement for Indo-Pakistanis at all. The average border guard can't tell the difference between an Arab and a Pakistani anyway, and as a lot of the South Asians have full British documents, it's really not a problem, even if they don't speak English, and a lot of them don't. But your average British customs officer can't tell the difference between spoken Arabic and say Punjabi, unless they come from one of those areas. Actually they can't tell the difference between Dutch and German either, hence the English word for the people from the Netherlands, the Dutch. But as the Dutch and Germans are both white and forrin they're open for investigation.'

'Are you suggesting that the British Customs officers are racist?'

'Heaven forefend! They're everything but. They *so* don't want to even be accused of racism, that the only people they will lean on are the people who look

English, but don't speak like an Englishman. If you're one of those they'll treat you like a spy, and ask you to explain the LBW law.'

'The LBW law?'

'It's a very complex rule in the very complex sport called cricket. You have to completely understand all the rules if you want to watch it. And the only people who do, had ancestors who were either British, or part of the British Empire. Most of the latter now take great pleasure beating the English at their own game. Anyway, if you're white and can explain the LBW law, you've got to be an Australian or a Kiwi. There's so much legitimate business trying to get through the Dover-Calais bottleneck at the moment, the poor customs officers are totally overloaded. Why should they be on the lookout for a criminal who's only done his monkey business in France, and who's probably never even been to England before?'

'So that's how Mehdi Arraq got out of the Europol zone? They shipped him to England. So what do we do about it?'

'Well sir,' Truchaud smiled. 'That all depends on how official you want things to be.'

'What do you mean?'

'Have you heard of the Old Friends' Network?'

'Yes, of course.'

'Well, I've got an old chum who works for The Thames Valley Constabulary, and he could really use a favour from us right now.'

'And you can vouch for this man?'

'Oh he's one of the best, no doubt about it.'

'And what does he want from us?'

'A spot of surveillance.'

'And what would we get in return?'

'Well I was planning on asking him if he would put his feelers out for our Mehdi Arraq, and if possible to pop him into a packing case in a truck coming through Dover-Calais, and let us know which one he's in, so once it's on the A26 it can be stopped and searched…'

'Not at the port?'

'At this moment, the outgoing customs are both on the British side of the tunnel. Remember, the Channel Tunnel was built and commissioned when the two countries were both in the EU and treating each other like friends and partners. We're still constructing a proper customs post on the French side of the size and capability to cope with the quantity of traffic coming in. I understand it will cover most of the thirty kilometres between Calais and Dunkirk, and will service the needs of both ports. We didn't think the Brits would actually go through with Brexit, I understand. Anyway we'll need the truck to be formally on French soil before we strip it down.'

'And nobody would be any the wiser?'

'And nobody will be any the wiser.'

'Go and do it, and don't let me know about it until you've done it. I'll look forward to your catching Mehdi Arraq. Can I come and watch you interrogate him?'

'It'll be my pleasure sir.'

§§§§

Gray sat at his desk in the flat, and grinned at Watts. 'Well that seems to have worked out okay.'

'So what's he want from us, guv?' the driver asked.

'Well there's an Algerian who has apparently snuck into Britain, and he's a person of interest in Paris. First thing we have to do is find him, and when they're ready for him, we pack him up in a crate and ship him back to France.'

'What did he do?'

'I think he was involved in a post office or two getting turned over. There was quite a lot of innocent blood spilled too. I gather he's not too bothered who gets caught in the crossfire.'

'Nice,' Watts commented and after a pause, he asked, 'Meanwhile?'

'Oh they already know where Philip Nicholson is hiding, and they're going to watch him for us, you know, find out where he goes, who he talks to. You know the sort of stuff. They're putting a hacker on his tail, so with a bit of luck and a following wind we'll find out who he's talking to in England. Once we know who he's talking to over here, we'll know who we've got to start recruiting here. We'll also hopefully find out when and where they're planning to do whatever it is that they're planning to do to the Prime Minister. I'll have a word with someone at Dover customs to see what info they've got on that Algerian that Truchaud wants found.'

'Will the Chief Constable be happy about you doing that, guv?'

'I'll tell her she'd better be,' said Gray and picked up the phone.

Watts was right, "Aunty Muriel" didn't catch on immediately to what he was suggesting. Doing a bit of search and locating someone for the French as a quid pro quo got round the difficult state international politics had got into right now but it took a little time to get the Chief Constable on side. However when the deal was coupled with free surveillance of Nicolson, she came on board. Anyway, as Gray remarked to his chief, if there are routes that illegals are using to come into the country at the moment, it wouldn't do us any harm to know something about it. The whole point of Brexit was surely to isolate Britain from the rest of Europe, or at least to know who is coming in, why and for how long they're planning on staying. Of course we want tourists to visit for a few weeks to spend the money they've earned abroad, and wealthy plutocrats to come over and buy up football clubs or whatever. Lots of successful football clubs, means lots of happy voters, and lots of happy voters…'

'Means loads and loads of votes. You're a very cynical young man,' "Aunt Muriel" had told him down the phone, but with a chuckle, and gave him permission to carry on with his plan. She even gave him permission to fund the cost of the hacker staying in the same hotel as Nicholson, which hadn't actually been one of Truchaud's requests, but Gray had floated it and it had wings. When he went back to Truchaud it would mean that the surveillance might actually work.

§§§§

Piet van Wijk sat in the restaurant at the Hotel Richebourg in the village of Vosne-Romanée, a couple of kilometres north of the small town of Nuits-Saint-Georges. It was the beating heart of Red Burgundy country and the menu in front of him was amazing. What was even more exciting; the wine list was huge. It was as big as a novella! Inspector Truchaud had even told him it was an "all-expenses-paid" trip. He looked at his phone, and drew up the pictures he had been sent by the inspector. He then looked across the room at the dapper middle-aged man at the table across the

31

room. Finally he looked back at his phone, satisfied. That was definitely his target. He then concentrated on the menu. *Œufs en Meurette* was a personal favourite of his. That would be his starter, followed by the sea bream and haricots, and some of the local cheeses to finish up with. The waiter took his order, and asked what he would like to drink. As an aperitif, a Kir was always something that had style and panache for him when he came to Burgundy. It was traditionally a sweet blackcurrant liqueur diluted down with a dry Aligoté white wine. Aligoté is very much the 'second' white grape in Burgundy, but perhaps in Brussels when he had asked for a Kir, they'd just mixed a slug of blackcurrant *siroop* with any old cheap dry white. To go with the meal, he had spotted a half-bottle of a wine he had always known about and wanted to try, but had never seen it on a menu before that moment; the Clos Blanc de Vougeot. This was a white Clos de Vougeot, and was the highest ranked white wine from the Côte grown north of Nuits Saint Georges. It was a Premier Cru, and as all connoisseurs of the games the Burgundians play will tell you, Premier Cru is the second rank of fine wines in Burgundy. The best three per cent are called Grand Cru. So this Clos Blanc isn't as grand as a Grand Cru perhaps, but all the Grands Crus from that area are red wines. He looked out of the window up the hill at a small walled vineyard up the slope. He had checked with Truchaud as soon as he heard the phrase, 'all-expenses-paid', and was told, 'within reason. If a bottle of Romanée-Conti appears on your bill, buster, you're on your own.' Hey ho, one day, he promised himself, he would taste the greatest, and most expensive wine in the world. The irony was that by looking though the window where he was sitting, he could see the vineyard where those grapes were growing. However a reasonably priced half-bottle of Le Clos Blanc would be well within the range of his allowance. After all he was under strict instructions to stay at that particular hotel in order to keep an eye on the strange Englishman across the room. And if he *was* staying at that particular hotel keeping an eye on that particular man, it would have been very obvious he was doing something odd, if he was sitting in the dining room and not having dinner. Stood to reason didn't it. 'I'll have a bottle of the Seventy five, he said looking at the list.' But just in case Nicholson was aware of him, he said the word Seventy-Five, the Walloon way, Septante-cinq, rather than the French way, Soixante-Quinze [Sixty-fifteen].

'Monsieur is from Switzerland?' the waiter asked politely.

'No, I'm from Belgium,' he replied. Hoping that if any quirks may appear in his behaviour then it would be attributed to his being Belgian.

The waiter brought back his Kir, and a plate with a couple of shot glasses on it, each with something in them that he hadn't ordered. The waiter explained that it was an '*amuse-bouche'*, a present from the chef. There was a tiny fork like a lobster pick on the plate beside it and there was also a small basket of warm fresh bread. He picked up his Kir, and sipped it. Oh yes that was more like it! He understood why it was the favourite aperitif of one Cardinal Kir after whom it was named. The Cardinal was the mayor of Dijon during the Second World War, and managed to keep things relatively calm during the occupation, so his favourite tipple was allowed to pass into current argot. It was cool, and had the dryness of the aligoté and the sweetness of the crème de Cassis.

Okay, so what was this thing that he had been sent to amuse his mouth? He picked up one of the shot glasses and the fork. He jabbed it into the shot glass. It went into the yellowish creamy liquid, about the consistency of English Custard and then into something much more solid. He pulled the fork out again, looked at the irregular looking black thing stuck on its tines, and realising that it was intended to amuse his mouth, rather than worry his eyes, he popped it onto his tongue. It was chewy, slightly meaty, and was very garlicky. And yes his mouth was sufficiently amused to try the other glass. It was another of the same. He then peeled a bit of bread and wiped the inside of the glass, to get what was left of the garlicky sauce out. Oh yes! His taste buds were now awake; he wondered what it was he had just eaten.

The waiter arrived with his little bottle of wine, and a rather large glass. He produced his waiter's friend corkscrew, cut off the top of the foil, and expertly withdrew the cork. He then passed the cork to van Wijk, who deciding that it was expected of him, sniffed at it. It smelled okay, but he didn't fully understand what, if anything, the cork should smell like. He supposed that that was the point. If the cork smelled mouldy, then he'd know about it quickly enough. He nodded, and the waiter put a little of the wine into the glass. The wine, a brilliant straw colour caught the sunlight pouring in through the dining room window, and glinted in the glass. He sniffed at it for a moment, and then swirled it round the glass as he had seen done so often before, and sniffed at it again. A fascinating collection of aromas came up from the glass. He could easily recognise the vanilla and toffee scents with a little fig and acacia honey coming in from behind. Oh, he hoped it wasn't going to be sweet, that wouldn't do any good to the fish. He took a mouthful, and sloshed it round his mouth. No it was pleasantly dry with a nice feeling in his mouth. Hmm. 'Very nice,' he said. He wondered whether the waiter was used to people saying that to him. The chances were that people drinking in that hotel would know about what wine was good, as opposed to just being rare and expensive.

'Satisfy my curiosity,' he continued, 'what was the *amuse-bouche*?'

'*Un Escargot en Aïöli,*' he replied smiling gently, obviously waiting for an expression of horror from a tourist who he had just eaten a snail in garlic mayonnaise.

There was going to be no such expression from him. So when the eggs en meurette arrived with a spoon, he was waiting for it with anticipation. Eggs lightly poached in red wine was something he had tried to do back home in Sint Niklaas, in Northern Belgium but had utterly failed at. There was obviously a trick to this, which he had yet to understand. These were perfect. The eggs and the wine were separated, but still runny. Perhaps they were put into the wine actually on the plate and were cooked separately. He would try to talk to the chef while he was still at the hotel, so that he could have some idea how to do it when he got back home.

Enjoying a mouthful of eggs he became aware that Nicholson was talking on his phone. Van Wijk looked at his own phone and watched it hunting down the numbers, both of Nicholson's phone and the one he was talking to. He was receiving a call from a local landline. Van Wijk noted them down, but he supposed his friend the inspector wouldn't be interested in them. Unlike the phone in Nicholson's pocket which had chosen that moment to go off too. It had received a text, and all of that also found its way into van Wijk's device. It was fortunate that the dining room was empty at the time, and in particular there were no teenagers in there. He remembered one time when he had been doing a surveillance job in a restaurant, and there were a couple of teenagers sitting together, but were communicating by texting rather than face to face conversation. It had made the results of the surveillance job of the day singularly difficult to unpick.

§§§§

Gray was looking carefully at the report. Exactly what it meant was uncertain, but it definitely showed that the game was afoot. 'Smilodon's in Britain,' was the message he was reading. Presumably the killer's code name was Smilodon, the scientists' name for the sabre-toothed cat. The fact that the beast was extinct did not fill him with hope. While it was alive, it was the largest and most powerful predator of its time. He had remembered that it became extinct relatively recently partly due to the fluctuating ice ages, and partly due to competition with humans over its food supply, being giant oxen, which were hunted to extinction themselves by the ever increasing numbers of homo not-very-sapiens. It is understood that the last Smilodon died a mere ten thousand years or so ago. If you were looking for a code name to be a powerful carnivore, it was a good one, particularly if you had been into prehistoric animals as Gray had been as a small boy. Moreover, unlike the T. Rex, it wasn't also the name of a pop group in the early seventies. Gray chuckled to himself about starting a rockabilly band just to call it the Sabre-Toothed Cats. In fact it was really only when Gray started finding girls interesting, that he stopped musing about how on earth the Stegosaurus successfully mated with all those bony plates sticking out from its back. The beast didn't have the brain power to think even simple ideas through like mechanics after all. Every dinosaur book he remembered had a line about the Stegosaurus having a brain the size of a walnut.

So 'Smilodon' was in Britain was he? That implied that he had been somewhere else before he came to Britain. The message didn't say anything else, just that he was on the British side of a border. There was no information as to where he had come from. The first and most obvious place was Scotland. The governments of Scotland and England were by now barely on speaking terms, and the unwillingness of the Westminster government to even talk about allowing the Scots to have a further referendum on independence was not helping the situation. Moreover the major revenue from Scotland's single major export, Scotch whisky, ended up in the English coffers, rather than staying in Scotland. Gray remembered when he was a lad he went round a distillery, and was made to feel very uncomfortable by the tour guide who described the tax collectors as "the English", and every time he said the word, he looked straight at Gray, and spat the word at him, dripping with contempt, as if he was the only English tourist in the place. But technically, Scotland was still in Britain, and the message didn't say that Smilodon was in England, so it was equally possible that s/he was hiding out in

Sauchie Hall Street at the moment. The very poor communications across Hadrian's Wall would certainly explain why a potential assassin might be a Scot.

Then again he might be a Welshman or an Irishman. The latter might be more likely, as the Irish had more recent exposure to a weapon culture. Or had he come in from Europe? And was he even a 'he'? Knowing the PM's proclivities, it might very well be a woman trying to honey trap him into breathing his last in a ditch. What sort of weapons would she use; herself?

The next question he found himself asking was, did the killer expect to get away with it, or was he or she going to go heroically down in flames, explaining to the public at large the reasons why the Prime Minister had been slain? If he was planning to get away with it, Gray mused, deciding that being politically correct and gender neutral was a waste of good thinking time; then lets face it; most killers are male, especially of the "Guns for Hire" variety. However, he thought, "Guns For Hire" did their killing for money, and not for some grand cause. Therefore if it were a commercial enterprise, it suggested that he would have a use for the cash after the event had taken place. You can't spend that money after you're dead or in custody. It suggested therefore that he would have some sort of exit strategy in place, or at least would have by the time the deed had been done. So assuming he was planning to not get caught, then that increased considerably the possibility of his not coming from the British Isles. Southern Ireland was an interesting idea; certainly he would be able to go to ground in Eire. However tight the border between the Irish states was, they hadn't built a wall, or an Iron Curtain between them, so it was still porous.

'Coming?' he asked Watts. 'We have to present

ourselves to the Home Secretary to justify our vast expenditure.' Watts grabbed his metaphorical chauffeur's cap and they were rapidly back in the Home Office. Watts parked the car and then enjoyed a coffee with the still apparently constipated desk Sergeant, while Gray was invited straight in when he tapped on the double door. Perhaps the Sergeant had let them know that he was on his way.

'Well?' asked the Home Secretary acidly. 'I have noticed singularly minimal recruiting so far, apart from the staff we've already provided for you. Do you have anything *at all* to tell us?'

She's sharp enough to cut yourself on the edges, Gray thought. 'Well, we've found Philip Nicholson, and he's informed us that there is a character codenamed Smilodon, who is already in Britain.'

'You've talked to him?' she asked, sounding very surprised.

'Not directly,' he replied, 'And I'm sure he has no idea that we are getting any information at all out of him. However, at this stage, we have no idea who Smilodon actually is or where he has come from, or what his plans are. At this stage therefore we're keeping Nicholson under close surveillance to see if he gives us anything else.'

'And who exactly is doing this surveillance?' asked a severe looking woman with a Scottish burr, who looked older than she probably would have liked. She was one of the Secretaries of State, sitting in the civilian row on Gray's left. It was a phrase that Gray had found gently amusing, 'Secretary of State'. He tried to imagine that rather brutish woman sitting over an old fashioned typewriter, and positively hammering its keyboard to pieces while trying to type a letter.

'I have a friend and partner in the Quai d'Orsay in Paris who's arranging the surveillance.' He looked the Home Secretary directly in the eye as he said that, to let her know that his misquote of one of the Prime Minister's famous three word slogans during the last general election and the subsequent abortive Brexit negotiations was intentional.

'Why?' chipped in the dry old Air Marshal from his right, the only one who still insisted on wearing a mask in the room, despite the social distancing in place. Gray idly wondered whether there were in fact several air force officers all fulfilling that role at different times, and simply made sure that they all wore the mask while they were in there. 'We haven't got any links with the French police at the moment. It's what Brexit was all about.'

'Britain may not have any links with France any more, but I still do,' Gray replied dryly. 'We are doing this as a sort of quid pro quo. We're looking out for a post office robber for them, who has apparently escaped into Britain through your "impenetrable" defences.' Gray was not going to be intimidated by these fools. He still had the case of the murdered journalist back home to go back to if they sacked him from this job, which he hadn't really wanted in the first place.

'Which explains the search and find that came out of your office yesterday evening,' said the Chief Constable, smiling. 'It has no direct links with your case?'

'You're absolutely right, ma'am,' Gray replied. 'The better results we can deliver to the French, the better help we can expect from them in return. Nicholson, so far, is our only lead.'

'And you trust this ah French policeman to come up with the goods?'

'Certainly, we worked together over a couple of transjurisdictional cases while Britain was still friends and partners with the French.'

'We still are friends and partners with the French,' protested the Secretary of State, getting increasingly annoyed with Gray's continuous hammering of the Prime Minister's three-word slogan over and over again, in much the same way as Gray had become fed up with it during the election itself.

'That's not how it feels on the streets ma'am,' Gray replied. 'Unless I am talking directly to Truchaud, I get nowhere at all. They are far from friendly.'

'Oh that's just the French being French.'

'And equally it's also the British being British. Fifty years of joint prosperity was smashed in an instant with Brexit. But I'm not here to argue politics with you, I'm here to brief you where we are so far. I'm also here to ask you if you have any sight of any plans the Prime Minister might have that would make him physically vulnerable.'

'I understand that the Right Honourable Gentleman is minded to take a few days holiday in Scotland with his fiancée soon,' she said, 'He's probably going to have a private chat with the First Minister on topics of mutual benefit like a repeat Independence Referendum.'

'Would he be tempted to walk among the electorate and press flesh?' Gray asked with growing alarm.

'Probably not,' the Home Secretary replied, 'But you never know. He does like hearing his name being shouted by fans in the street.'

'Does he actually want to end up dead in a ditch this

time? We'll need to know an exact schedule of any possible public appearances that he does plan to make before he gets out of bed each morning.'

'We will attempt to do that, but as nobody in this room is sleeping with him, it might be a little difficult to achieve that.'

Gray let out a dry chuckle, which was instantly picked on by the Secretary of State, 'What's so funny?'

'Oh nothing.'

'I said, "What's so funny?"'

'Well I was thinking that one or two of you ladies present ought to consider it as a future duty for the country, to sleep with the Prime Minister. From what I understand, the men in the room are not suitably qualified for the job. But he himself is not particularly selective provided his company is, erm, of the distaff persuasion.'

'Well you did ask for that,' said the Chief Constable looking across the table at the seething Secretary of State, who was sounding ever more Scottish the higher her hackles rose.

'Is there anything else?' Gray asked, 'because if not, I have a French robber to look for, and a French detective to talk to.' And without further ado he stood up and left the room.

§§§§

When he got back to the semi Polly greeted him with a, 'There was a French Detective asking for you five minutes ago. He asked if you would call him right back.' She passed a mobile across to him. 'Oh and by the way, Inspector Anson's in the living room.'

'What's he doing there?'

'Watching telly, I shouldn't wonder.'

Gray pressed the automatic redial, and when he was answered, he said 'Gray,' into the mouthpiece.

'Truchaud,' came the reply, 'Your Monsieur Nicholson has just checked out of the Richebourg Hotel, and for the moment, we're not sure where he's gone.'

'What? Just like that?'

'*Tout d'un coup.*' Came the reply. 'He had just received a telephone call, and he was up and off.'

'Did your man register that call?'

'Yes, it was the mobile with the same number as last night's call.'

'*Merde,*' said Gray, politely swearing in French to include Truchaud in the conversation. 'I think we have a spy in the Home Office.'

'I'm glad you have come to the same conclusion; if you hadn't I would have found the next part of the conversation a little embarrassing. It does mean your spy is also working against the French. I assume you explained your relationship with me and mine, and what we are doing together?'

'What, you mean looking for your Algerian in all the wrong places?'

'Exactly. Now I will certainly get back onto Europol to find your man Nicholson again, and recommence surveillance. We need to prove to your metropolitan police that we are better than you at finding people who don't want to be found.'

Gray let out a sigh of relief. He thought for a moment that since Nicolson had slipped his leash, he was now going to be on his own. It was not the case, but he did have to find a certain Algerian for Truchaud. 'Leave it with me,' the Frenchman said. 'I have one or two irons in the fire.'

Gray walked through into the living room. Anson was dozing in one of the armchairs. He woke up very smartly when Gray coughed.

'How you doing?' Anson asked.

'What do you know about a man who calls himself Smilodon?' Gray asked.

Anson thought for a moment and said, 'Not a lot.' He got out a notebook and pencil and scribbled the word down, and then scribbled a bit more. Putting on a faintly Irish accent he said, 'Son o' mild?'

'What are you doing?' Gray asked.

'Trying to see if it anagrams for us, but I can't see anything obvious.'

Gray wasn't sure what this fellow was taking, but as he was offered as a free good, he waited to see what he had come up with next.

'Smilo from Doncaster,' he burbled, 'Maybe S.M.I. from London, bit of a stretch I know, but I'll get someone onto it. You never know something may come out of it. What is it?'

'It's the technical name for the Sabre-Toothed Tiger,' Gray replied.

'Nasty,' Anson replied, 'Still if you've got to give yourself a predator as a code name, that's as good as any.'

'Except it's extinct.'

'Yes there is that. Well, leave it with me.' Anson got up and left the room. Moments later Gray heard the front door open and shut. What a peculiar fellow, he thought.

§§§§

'There's a DS Sharp on the phone for you, guv,' Polly announced jerking Gray out of his reverie, and passing the phone over.

'Hi there,' said Gray into the device. 'How you doing kiddo?'

'I'm fine,' said the pleasantly rustic female voice, who added, 'as always.'

'So why do I have the pleasure?'

'Well you remember the Sierra Nicholls case, that you left for us to get on with because you had found something more interesting and important to do.' Her voice carried just enough lightness of tone to tell him she was being ironic.

'Yes,' he said slowly in a rising semitone, implying an added, 'go on.'

'Well we're beginning to get somewhere.'

'That's good. Does it help me in any way? Are you telling me that they can't do without me, and they need me back now, or even sooner?'

'Err, not that no. Are you free to pop over sometime soon, we've had some photos you might find interesting dropped off by the paparazzo who took them.'

He looked at Watts over the top of the phone. 'What's the situation about me driving the car, re insurance and stuff?'

'Have you been passed out on it by a Police Instructor?' he asked.

'You know I haven't. I didn't even know those souped up devices existed until you showed me some of its potential.'

'Well, then I can't let you have the keys,' he replied. 'However, I can drive you wherever it is you want to go.'

'Is it okay for you to drive me over to Bucks with the blues and twos on?'

'Your every wish is my command, o revered leader.' Watts grinned.

'In which case, we're going out. I'll grab all the active phones.' He put his mouth back to the phone. 'See you in about half an hour at the Royal Oak?' He said to the voice at the other end.

'The Royal Oak it is, guv,' came back to him. The Oak is a pub just down the road from the Police Station which had been Gray's headquarters, and is a place where a great many of the local police have lunch, and also where they have any number of 'unofficial' meetings. The pub seems to have been designed with clandestine meetings in mind. He glanced at Polly. 'You can always find me on my phone,' he said, 'I don't expect we'll be very long.'

The car burbled out of the street, but once it hit the M4 Watts gave it its head. With its blue lights flashing in its radiator grille, and its headlights on as well, the car showed what it thought of the concept of a 'speed limit'. It may have been the fastest anyone had travelled on an English open road, since the then reigning Formula One world champion Mike Hawthorn came face to face with reality on the Guilford By-Pass over sixty years before.

Gray travelled most of the way with his eyes shut. If Watts were to ask, he would say he was just snoozing, but the reality was that he was utterly terrified. It wasn't that he was frightened by Watts' driving, but it was all the other half-wits on the road who might be texting on their phones in front of them, and might just get in their way. Those were the drivers who really terrified him.

The Royal Oak was traditionally warm when you walked through the door. It smelled of Yorkshire pudding and an oak fire, even though there wasn't one to be seen. The Inglenook fireplace had a table set in it, and at that table sat a familiar face in mufti. She had a pleasant as opposed to a pretty face. It wasn't one of those faces that grabbed your attention, as soon as you entered a room; but once you had clocked it, you wondered why it hadn't. Her features were even, with a light dusting of freckles over her nose, and her shortish brown hair was slightly wavy, but nevertheless organised. She wore no obvious war paint. Gray had always liked her and her rustic accent. He formally introduced DS Sharp and Watts to each other, and asked the pair of them what they wanted to drink.

'I'm driving, guv,' said Watts.

'Oh that's what you called it,' Gray replied drily. 'So what'll you have?'

'A Muddy Water,' he replied.

Gray and Sharp exchanged glances, 'What's that?' they both said simultaneously.

'Orange juice and coke, fifty-fifty mix.'

'Orange juice and Coke it is,' he turned to the DS, who waved a hand at the wine glass in front of her, which was still nearly full. 'Next time,' he said, and walked over to the bar.

'Orange Juice and Coke and a pint of bitter please.'

The kid behind the bar who probably was old enough to be working behind a bar, but not a lot older than that, took a bit of persuading which components were to be mixed with which, and what was to go into a glass on its own. When he had finally created a Muddy Water, he handed it across to Gray and asked him whether it looked right. It was a brown cloudy most unattractive looking mixture with a few bubbles scantily rising to the surface. 'Does that look right?' he asked with a slightly bewildered expression on his thin angular face.

'I haven't the faintest idea,' he replied, 'I'll ask.'

He carried the glass over to the table. Watts took a mouthful, 'Spot on!' he said.

'It looks disgusting,' Sharp remarked drily.

'It looks like a Guinness with a couple of shots of Pernod mixed in,' Watts replied, 'a real drinker's concoction.'

Gray went back to the bar and said, 'Des seems to like it.'

'Des?'

'The Designated Driver. Looks like it might be a worthwhile trick to have up your sleeve these days. How much do I owe you?' Gray paid up and took his pint back to the table and sat down.

'So Sergeant Watts here tells me he works with you now at the Met.'

Oh he's a Sergeant is he? Nice to know. I hope she doesn't want to know his forename too. That could be embarrassing.

'Susie tells me you used to work with her round here,' said Watts grinning. He had certainly never known Detective Sergeant Suzette Sharpe as 'Susie'. They'd always referred to her as "Becky" behind her back, after the character in Vanity Fair. "Susie" would surely have suggested a progression in a relationship in a direction that neither of them had ever intended.

'So, DS Sharpe,' he said formally with a little chuckle in his voice. 'You said you had some pictures I might be interested to see.'

'Yes. You know Sierra Nicholls was a freelance journalist. Well, earlier on the day she died, she had a working lunch with the Prime Minister and his, "ah-consort" at *La Coupole* to do a pre-election interview. Everything's a pre-election something at the moment isn't it?'

'Has been that way for at least the last couple of years,' he replied.

'Now on those sort of occasions, she usually had a pet Paparazzo squirrelled away to get the odd candid snapshot to accompany the interview in the press for whoever had commissioned it, and this occasion was no exception. What was, however, a little different was that she was accompanied herself, so the dinner party appeared to be made up of two couples. Well Giovanni, the paparazzo, who was not the man with Sierra on his arm incidentally, has let us have his pictures once he heard what happened to her. Well we've searched high and low, but nobody has the vaguest idea who the hell the man accompanying Sierra actually is.'

'He's not in her address book?'

'Nor, as far as we can tell, is he on her phone. He isn't on any of the official press registers either.'

'No photographic record on any computer database?'

'Nothing that we have found no.'

'Anyway we got to ask the PM and his, "ah-consort" who he was. We got the reply that he was introduced to them, but "I, ah, don't remember his name, nor does the old girl, but he did seem a frightfully good sort, and he certainly helped that little poppet Sierra get the interview she wanted." He didn't think he was English, "probably French, something like that, an acceptable sort of foreigner, spoke perfect English; only had a slight accent.'"

'May I see the pictures?' Gray asked, gently amused by her imitation of the Prime Minister's voice.

He flipped through the photos. 'They're copies,' said Sharp, 'so you can keep them.' Gray continued thumbing through them. He was amused to see that the lion's share of the pictures were of Sierra herself, and the short skirt she was almost wearing. They were taken from all around the room, so apart from the obvious ones of the Prime Minister and the journalist in deep conversation, no doubt one of which would have accompanied the article when she sold it, there were a number of excellent pictures in sharp focus of the unnamed man in deep conversation with the PM's 'ah-consort'. He wondered what they had to talk about. He also thought it would be instructive as far as his new job was concerned, to see whether he might have any interesting suggestions as to what the Prime Minister's movements might be over the coming weeks.

'Well, that's why I thought you might be interested in the pictures,' said "Becky". 'To us he's a person-of-interest in our murder enquiry, but we also thought he might be useful in your investigation as well.'

'So that I too might be on the lookout for this elusive Frenchman?'

'Exactly, and if you run him to ground, you might allow us to take a crack at him too.' She tossed a USB stick at him. 'All the pictures are on there too,' she added. 'We have promised the paparazzo we won't sell them or publish them, but for some reason we didn't promise him we wouldn't copy them or give them to our law enforcement colleagues. Can't imagine why we forgot to do that.'

§§§§

'Well? What did you think of that?'

'I assume, guv, that you're not asking for my opinion on the Detective Sergeant,' said Watts who was driving much more sedately on his return journey into London. He was obviously not so keen to get back to work either.

'Of course not, Becky's an old friend and colleague.'

'Amuses me that you think of her as a Becky which she isn't, rather than as a Susie, which she is, but that's how nicknames work isn't it. I was always known as "Killer" Watts, not after any homicidal tendencies I might or might not have but after the unit of power, the Kilowatt/Hour. They thought it was funny at the time, and I didn't object unduly. There were many less amusing nicknames attached to some of our mates that I didn't care too much about mine; I mean poor old Hancock's nickname drove him out of the force. Anyway, as we were saying, you realise she's recruited us, don't you, guv?'

'Huh?'

'She's making sure you're on the lookout for their mysterious Frenchman, and if you find him, at the very least she's expecting you to tip her the nod.'

'Well when we get back to base, we'll have to ask our friend Truchaud if he has any idea who he is. It's always possible he's on a French database, to which we no longer have any access over here.'

When they pulled up at the house, Polly was still there sitting in front of the television in the living room. There was a row of silent phones sitting beside her on the sofa.

'Anything happened while we were out?' Gray asked her.

'Naa, only the Chief Constable checking up to find out whether there was someone here to answer the phone, and she asked whether you needed anything. I said you didn't at this moment in time, but I'd ask you if the sitch had changed, when you got back.'

'Was she annoyed we weren't here?'

'I said you had your reasons, and mine not to reason why.'

Gray smiled. This kid would do. He just hoped that the other two he hadn't yet met were as good. He pulled out "Becky's" memory stick and stuck it in one of his laptop's sockets. He pulled up its menu and picked on a PDF at random. It pulled up a picture of Sierra Nicholls in full laugh. It was a poignant thought that three hours after that moment of laughter, she would be dead. He wondered if it was a real laugh, or if she was just acting for the Prime Minister. He then looked through the others until he had found a clear picture of the mystery man. He dialled Truchaud.

'We have an interesting problem,' he told the Frenchman. 'While assisting my colleagues on a murder case, we have come upon a person unknown; who we're informed spoke with a French Accent. He hasn't shown up on any of our databases, and we wondered whether we could run it through yours.

'Send it over,' said Truchaud. 'You've still got my e-mail address haven't you.'

'I have if you haven't changed it.'

Gray pinged it over and waited for Truchaud to look at it and call him back.

He didn't have to wait long; Truchaud was back to him almost instantly. 'You know who that is, don't you?'

'Haven't the faintest idea,' he replied.

'Well, I'm very impressed. That's Mehdi Arraq, the person we asked you to look for. Where is he? Can you get him into France by tomorrow? Any way you like, although we'd rather he was in a fit state to answer all our questions however, if it's all the same to you. Bruised, we can cope with, badly broken, not so much.' Truchaud sounded positively excited.

'Ah, hang on a moment. Firstly, we've got no idea where he actually is right now, and if we did know, you have to understand that he is a person of interest in an on-going murder case of our own, so we need him to answer our questions when we find him. If he ends up formally arrested for the crime over here, we'll let you know, and we'll no doubt come to some agreement how to proceed from there. Just to fill you in, ours is a definitely murder case.'

'By all means interrogate him first, but once you've finished with him, don't let him go; pop him into a packing case and ship him off to France. We need him too.'

'You've got it.'

'Meanwhile, we've found your Peter Nicholson again. He's holed up in a hotel on the Rhine in Germany.'

'He likes his wine regions doesn't he?'

'I don't know much about the wine round there…' Truchaud started.

'Because it's not Burgundy you mean?'

'Yes, something like that. Anyway, he's in a hotel called the Schloß Adler, up on the top of a cliff overlooking the river. It's apparently a golf and hunting hotel, and very upmarket.'

'You mean the people who stay there take pot shots at the golfers on the green?'

'Yes, and the golfers try to hit the hunters with a tee shot from the fifth. I haven't the faintest idea to be honest. However we've got someone on their way there to act surveillance on him.'

'Not the same man?'

'Of course not, even your Nicholson would probably realise something was up if he saw the same Belgian across the dining room on the Jakobsburg.'

The phone buzzed and Gray picked it up again. 'Anson here,' came a voice.

'Hi there,' Gray replied, 'what have you got?'

'Well, We've found someone who may be of interest,' he said.

'Go on.'

'There's a fellow called Stuart Maxwell Ingram, who has been under investigation by special branch recently.'

'Why?'

'Well he seems to be involved in a fake passport ring.'

'How do you mean?'

'Well they investigated his home recently and when they went in they found all sorts of passports with his face on, but with different names, and birthplaces. However when they investigated those passports it turned out that the passport office had genuinely created all of them. You know, birth certificate, address etcetera. So the Special branch people got interested like they do, and found that the birth certificates were absolutely genuine, but were for someone who had been dead a long time. You know a kid is born, gets registered, gets something nasty and dies, and that's that, except that thirty years later Ingram gets a copy of the birth certificate, maybe the real one even, and applies for a passport with it.'

'Very tricky,' said Gray. 'So where is this man at the moment?'

'Well,' said Anson down the phone, 'There's the rub. Nobody seems to know. He appears to have vanished off the face of the earth.'

'Get looking for him,' said Gray, 'and as soon as you locate him, get in touch with me. I want to have a word with him.

§§§§

Ingrid Schneider was waiting for her dining companion in the bar. She was a middle-aged woman slightly greying round the edges, and dressed as if she had been recently widowed. Certainly she bore no resemblance to the sort of person who might be a hacker. She was simply too old for that sort of thing. Moreover she was nursing a glass of Federweiss, with a certain lack of confidence in the glass's contents. The liquid was cloudy, with a few tiny bubbles in it. It was a glass of the new raw unfiltered wine of the year. The cloudiness was caused by the yeast still in the wine continuing the fermentation. She understood that it had been drawn from the barrel by the winemaker that morning into the earthenware jug from which it had just been poured. She doubted that it was the vintner's best wine, and was probably from a fairly ordinary cuvée, that he saved just for making Federweiss. That jug would probably cease to be served in the bar after lunch, and would go straight into the kitchen from there if there was any left, where it would be filtered and added to the salad dressing for the evening meal. Another jug would no doubt appear from the vineyard that evening.

Nicholson, her target, was already in the bar when she arrived. The mugshot she had been sent by Europol had been a pretty good one, and there was no doubt that the man in front of her was the mark. Once again he had received a message, to which he had replied. She sent all of them back to Commander Truchaud in Paris, and waited for further instructions.

§§§§

'Just thought you'd like to know that we've received a message from the Jakobsburg,' Truchaud's voice came out of the phone.

'It doesn't take very long to get back there does it,' replied Gray drily.

'How about letting him trip himself up?' Said Truchaud.

'What do you mean?'

'Send a message ostensibly from him to the spy this end which will require a reaction. With a bit of luck we'll at least catch the spy, and while we think we've identified your Algerian, we're not far off sorting the whole thing out.'

'Okay,' said Gray. 'What do you suggest?'

'Let me think on it,' said Truchaud. 'I'll call you back shortly.' And disconnected the call.

Gray wandered into the kitchen. At the table Polly and Watts were sitting laughing at something one of them had said.

'Morning, guv,' said Polly. 'You look in need of a cup of Java.'

'You read my mind disturbingly well,' he replied. 'Have you been here all night? I thought you kids worked in shifts.'

'Got back in fifteen minutes ago. You've just missed Tracy. She's gone off home now.' She was making herself busy with the cafetière, and Gray looked at those piercings she had in her face and hands. He couldn't help wondering whether they hurt. They certainly howled, 'I'm a masochist,' at him. Her features would certainly have been softer without them. He spanked the source of the thought that had come automatically into his head about her walking past a powerful electromagnet, and it pulling her whole face off. It simply appalled him what ridiculous thoughts entered his head uninvited from time to time, and here was yet another he would never voice in public.

'Guv,' she said looking up quizzically, with an expression that really didn't suit the metalwork in her face. 'Can you do me a favour and not mention the job we're actually doing here to my dad if you meet him?'

'Two questions, firstly, when am I likely to meet him? And Two, you do realise this is a highly classified operation, so nobody should be blabbing anything about the operation to your dad.'

'That's good, cos as you will probably realise my dad is not in favour of Brexit Boris, and if he knew someone had killed him, he would be more likely to celebrate rather heavily than get him arrested, especially after all that postal vote stuff.'

'What postal vote stuff?' Gray was genuinely confused.

'Well at that last election there were ten times as many postal votes as there had ever been before. Right? Now was that pattern a general trend all over the country, or was it in somewhere in particular?'

'I don't know.'

'Next question my dad asked me, cos he thinks I'm an actual policeman, just because I work for the police. Sometimes the finer points of stuff just go over his head. Anyway, as I was saying, you know the postal votes are counted at the same time as the ordinary votes after the polling stations close on election day. Right?'

'So I believe.'

'So how did that foreign secretary bloke know that the large number of postal votes coming in was good for his party. Also how did that BBC reporter girl with the lopsided grin know that the Tories had done well out of the postal votes before they had been counted?'

'I have a feeling you're going to give me an explanation.'

'Well my dad says the only way that they could have known so much about the results of what came out of the postal vote system at that particular time, and you have to say they pretty much got it on the nail, was if they knew what had actually gone into the postal ballot boxes in the first place.'

'Is your dad accusing the government of stuffing the ballot boxes? I think the phrase is Electoral Fraud.'

'Well, you know my dad…'

'No.'

'Well cut him in half and you'd see the word "Labour" like in a stick of Blackpool Rock. He likes to know everything is on the up and up, especially when he's lost, and to quote him, "That one didn't smell right."'

'I'll mention your point when I'm next chatting to someone in the Crown Prosecution Service. You know we've even got a senior member in the group in the Home Office.'

'Would you, guv? I'm sure my dad would appreciate it. Anyway, guv' she said stirring the cafetière, 'What's a-happening with our case?'

'We've got to think up a message to send back up the line, to find out who in the Home Office is not on our side.'

'Well they're all politicians; so they're all on their own side aren't they? Stands to reason, guv. All got their trotters in the trough, s'what my dad always says.'

'So how would your dad catch a politician with his trotters in the trough?'

'Give him an incentive he can't resist. Politicians is suckers for incentives, my dad always says.'

'Any bright ideas?' Watts joined in the fun.

'How about sending a fake message from your smiley old Don to one of those numbers we already have,' Polly suggested.

'How do you mean?'

'Well something like, "they're on to me, pull me out."'

'Well there's a problem there. How will we know if he's actually pulled out? If we assume he's gone into hiding, and he still goes ahead. But I like your thinking.'

'How about if instead we try to get the spy to identify himself?' suggested Watts. 'After all we're presumably sure that the spy's based in the Home Office.'

Gray thought about it for a moment. 'Better,' he said. Let's think that through. If we can disconnect the spy from Smilodon, that would help.

Gray was still thinking hard to himself. Firstly who was it more important to catch, the spy in the Home Office, or Smilodon himself? Surely it went without saying that if he had to pick one and one only to catch, it would be Smilodon., and the best route to catch Smilodon would surely be through the Spy, who's apparently in direct contact with him. If Truchaud's hackers' reports were anything to go by, and now Smilodon's a person of interest in a murder case, he can be hunted down hard for something he's already done and not just for something he might do in the future.

So how do we up the ante?

Well perhaps letting the spy know that he's getting a bit anxious might have an interesting effect. He wondered whether those messages they had contained some sort of code that might validate its source. Is there some sort of strange word order that might identify him? Does he split an infinitive just to show it really is him? Did they have enough of his messages yet for an analyst to assess if he has a pattern that he conforms to? Might be worth having an analyst of our own based here as a full member of the team. That's something to look into.

§§§§

'I think your man Nicholson has got the wind up,' said Truchaud down the phone. 'He's sent a message back to your spy to pull Smilodon out.'

'Well that tells me that Nicholson hasn't got any direct contact with Smilodon, but the spy presumably has.'

'Just exactly what do we know?' Truchaud asked thoughtfully.

'Well as far as we understand it Nicolson was behind the plot to blow up Downing Street, and when there was one missing casualty from that plot, he decided to go into hiding and plot another attempt to complete the package.'

'Okay, and he got out of Britain before anyone knew they were looking for him, and ended up hiding in France.'

'Meanwhile the Prime Minister dragged Britain out of the EU by the scruff of its neck, so co-operation between the various police forces and the British security services stopped on the spot. Good thing we're friends isn't it, and we're both willing to speak each other's language. What does your man Watts think of your having long telephone conversations in French?'

'I expect he understands everything we're saying. A very capable human being is our Sergeant Watts. If the job requires I talk to the French Police, he would expect me to do so in the way that works best.'

'And his politics?'

'I have no idea; I don't suppose he has either. Anyway Nicholson is hiding in Germany talking to plotters on cell phones. From what I understand he has a number of phones with him, each of which is connected to one person only. Presumably they're all in the UK. One of those UK phones is in the pocket of someone quite high up in the Home Office. We know that because things that I have discussed in those meetings have got back to Nicholson by the time I have got back to the flat. What we don't know is who it is.'

'But you've got their number?'

'Oh yes, we got that from Nicholson's phone, and I called it from one of our burners, but there was no reply.'

'May I suggest that that was because the number

wasn't either Nicholson's number, or Mehdi's number, both of which the phone would recognise and identify?'

'So if we can get Nicholson's number plugged into one of our phones, then it might think it was Nicholson on the other end and speak to us?'

'That's the idea.'

'And if that phone goes off in the Home Office, while I'm dialling it, it will give away the identity of the Spy?'

'Worth a try.'

§§§§

'Technical?' said the voice.

'Inspector Gray here from the Home Office Task Force. What can you do for me to make a copy of a phone. We've got it's number, and we know it's coming in from Germany. It's talking to a number somewhere in London, but we don't know where. Any bright ideas?'

'Well we could make the London handset think it was talking to Germany, while it is in fact talking to you. We then put a tracker on the phone you've got and see where that one's located.'

'Sounds great, when can you have this done by?'

'Seeing it's you and you're on top priority, probably have it at your door in about six hours.'

'Better and better.'

§§§§

When he woke up the following morning, he was greeted by the ubiquitous Polly, who had once again just got back in. 'Yeah Miff was 'ere last night when a uniform delivered the package said to give it to you as soon as you got up. Got coffee on the go if you're interested.'

'Go for it,' he said unwrapping the little parcel like it was a long awaited birthday present. It was a small cellphone, which he tapped and it came alive. The box had a loose piece of paper inside it on which was written 'password Sabre6'. He pressed the start-up button, and filled in the code word and the screen lit up. The phone was fully charged, and there was one number programmed into its memory. 'I wonder whether they expect me to eat this bit of paper,' he mumbled, 'Does this look like rice paper to you?' he asked Polly.

'Rice paper?' Polly replied with another question, 'What's that?'

He realised it was a considerable time since he had seen a traditional macaroon with an almond sunk into the top and a rice paper bottom. The twenty-first century has changed a great many things, he thought.

At the next meeting in the Home Office, Gray put his plan in motion. They were all sitting around the table and Watts, sitting outside in the waiting room dialled the Spy's cellphone with their specially prepared phone. There was silence in the big room. Gray reckoned he had pretty good hearing, but he couldn't hear a phone vibrating against skin or the contents of a handbag or pocket. Nada. Disappointed after briefing the Home Office about various leads, some of which were true, some of which not so, just to confirm at least that the Spy had been in the room. The hacker in the Schloβ Adler, would then report back to Nicholson what had been said.

Driving back to the flat with the phone now ensconced in Gray's pocket, he was surprised to hear it ring. He opened it and listened. It was a full report to Nicholson of what he had said in his report, and Nicholson's reply. It appeared that the technical wizards had created a perfect clone of Nicholson's phone. He prayed there were no extraneous noises from his end going into the mix. London Traffic noise would be a dead giveaway. Once the conversations clicked off, he shut the phone. 'I think we've had a breakthrough,' he said to Watts.

§§§§

Ingrid Schneider had always been a very patient woman, and right now she was quite happy just to sit in the Schloß Adler bar and watch the world go by, or in the particular case of Philip Nicholson, stay still. He was certainly appearing increasingly anxious by the apparent lack of activity on his phones. She was wondering whether something should have happened by now, and it hadn't. She had eaten her lunch, and was now sitting in the bar drinking coffee. She wasn't sure that she wanted to have another glass of Federweiss again ever, even if it came from a new batch. The dregs of her aperitif glass had been quite unpleasant. The first mouthful had been flowery and delicate, the final one had been sour and earthy, maybe even faeculent. Her companion had joined her for lunch, but being younger and fitter, had gone off for a walk in the woods. Ingrid was not sure that that had been such a good idea, she was fairly sure there were hunters in the woods, after all it was a *Golf und Jagdhotel* and the thought of trigger happy *Jäger* wandering round the same woods, armed to the teeth looking for anything that moved alarmed her. Gerti assured her that her Day-Glo over-jacket *should* offer adequate protection. Ingrid replied that it just made her a more obvious target. As far as she was concerned she would need to be wearing nothing less than a full sized battle tank before she would be tempted to roam around those woods, considering some of the weapons she had seen. But anyway she was working, and she was relieved to see that Nicholson shared similar views about the wood as her.

A text dropped into Nicholson's phone and he looked at it, with an expression of increasing concern. After a moment, he texted back. Ingrid could feel those conversations taking place in her phone where it lay against her left thigh. She didn't react, and took a sip of coffee. It was only after a further response had come back into Nicholson's phone, and he then got up and walked out of the room, that Ingrid took a look at her device.

She looked at both comments. Once again he was telling his contact, presumably in London, to pull the assassin out.

Nicholson: Pull him out. Just exactly that, it read no more, no less.

Contact: He won't be happy.

Nicholson: I don't care. I want the operation cancelled.

Contact: Are we going to pay him anyway?

Nicholson: He's already got his half share up front.

Contact: As I said, he won't be happy, his comment yesterday was that most of his up front money had already been spent on the equipment to do the job.

Nicholson: So he won't have to buy it for his next

job, whatever that might be.

At that point Nicholson had walked out of the bar. Ingrid had wondered whether she had been compromised, as he only seemed to send messages when he was in her line of sight, but maybe her phone wouldn't catch a text that wasn't being communicated fairly close to her. Anyway she sent the messages off to Commander Truchaud in Paris.

§§§§

'She thinks she may have been made,' said Truchaud. 'Do any of those comments look like a smokescreen to you?'

'I think we'll know in twenty-four hours if Nicholson disappears again,' Gray replied. 'I'll keep a very close eye on what goes on our end. If he has caught on to what we're doing, then it may be that he's trying to make us relax. Do you think he has another way of contacting Smilodon, so that he knows to ignore what's going on at the moment? Does, for example, Nicholson speak Arabic?'

'We do know for sure that Nicholson is the front man of this operation?' Truchaud mused down the phone.

'If he isn't then we're all doomed aren't we?' Gray replied drily. 'If there's a completely different plot going on, and we've missed the point of the whole thing, then whoever is the target is in serious trouble.'

Gray was feeling increasingly uncomfortable about the whole thing. Maybe the best thing to do right now would be to identify the Spy and bring him or her out into the open. If the Spy was the only link between Smilodon and the rest of 'the Committee', then breaking that link would disrupt something.

'Have we got a phone here that will mimic Smilodon's phone?' he asked.

Polly rummaged around on the table, 'I think that'll be the one,' she said producing a rather old looking black Nokia with protruding buttons. It wasn't even a flip phone.

'You're sure?' he asked.

She pressed one of its buttons and the tiny screen at the top lit up for a moment. She tapped one or to other buttons, and then turned it off again. 'That's the one,' she said confidently.

'And it's got the Spy's number programmed in?' he asked.

''S'what I was checking for, she replied.

Gray dropped it in his pocket. 'Good,' he said, and rummaging in his pocket, he pulled out the phone the Police Commissioner had given him. 'Hello, is that Aunt Muriel?' he asked.

'Hello Gray,' came back down the slightly poor quality line, 'What can I do for you?'

'Can you spare me a couple of uniformed police in the next half hour. Fairly impressive types. I want them to make an arrest.'

'Oh who?'

'I don't know yet, but if they come here in about twenty minutes, I'll brief them.'

'And where is this arrest going to take place?'

'The Home Office.'

'What?'

'You'll see it all happen, see you in about half an hour.' He disconnected.

Ten minutes later a police car pulled up, and two uniformed officers knocked at the Front door. 'Come in gentlemen,' said Watts, who was the first up to open it. 'The guv'nor's in here.' He led them into the living room.

The smaller of the two men, wearing the uniform of an inspector spoke first. 'So what's all this about sir?'

'Did the Commissioner brief you at all?' Gray replied.

'Well she did say that there's a plot afoot to kill the PM and you're trying to stop it. Are we going to arrest the assassin?'

'Sadly not so much,' Gray replied 'The person you're going to arrest is someone who knows who the assassin is, and is in direct contact with him.'

'So who is this person?'

'I don't know yet, but we all will in about half an hour.' He tossed the phone that Polly had just given him to the inspector. 'You'll need that,' he added.

'And where are we going?' asked the huge bull necked sergeant beside him.

'The Home Office,' Gray replied.

The sergeant produced a big meaty grin. 'The 'ome office eh? That'll do.' Obviously the man-mountain had problems with bureaucracy, and this was something he had looked forward to for a very long time.

'All you have to do is dial that number in that phone, as soon as I have gone into the council chamber. After a while it will no doubt be disconnected. Once it has been disconnected redial it. Keep redialling it until I personally come out and tell you to stop.'

The Inspector passed the phone to the sergeant, 'I get the feeling you're really going to enjoy this job Sergeant,' he said.

This time the sergeant's grin widened even further and displayed a moderately complete set of teeth. He had obviously done some boxing in the past. 'Yes, guv,' he said happily.

'Watts and I will go in our car, if you can follow us in yours. Don't be too conspicuous; we don't want our prisoner to be aware until whatever goes down is actually doing so.

§§§§

Gray and Watts trotted up the steps to the side door of the Home Office. The same rather sad uniformed Sergeant was behind the desk. Gray wondered whether they had cloned him, in much the same way he wondered whether the Commissioner had cloned his Pollies. In both cases they were the only ones he ever saw.

'Stay here Watts, and keep an eye open. When the Inspector arrives, show them into the anteroom, and get that Sergeant dialling.'

'Guv', came the reply.

Gray walked through the door and parked himself at the end of the table. The Commissioner threw him a look, but the look he returned said simply, 'not yet.'

'Well,' said the Home Secretary from the far end of the table, 'Inspector Gray, what do you have to report?'

'Well the French Police and I have come up with a likely candidate for the assassin. Moreover we think it is the same person that the Thames Valley Police are looking for concerning the murder of Sierra Nicholls.'

'The journalist?' came a Scottish voice from the civilian side of the table.

'That's the one,' he replied, 'Did you know her?'

'I think she interviewed me once on my way up,' came the slightly arrogant reply from the Attorney General. Gray shuddered slightly inside. He really didn't like that woman. He really hoped it was her he was going to arrest.

His phone vibrated against his thigh. He glanced at it. It was a text from Watts, which read, 'The Sergeant's dialling.' He pressed the acknowledged button and dropped it back in his pocket.

'Anything important Chief Inspector?' asked the Home Secretary acidly, 'Counter-terrorist criminal activity perhaps?' It was against protocol to do anything with a mobile phone while the committee was in session. Mobile phones had been a recent invention, while the Home Office Committee was centuries old, and was still trying to catch up with the eighteenth century.

'No Ma'am just the wife,' he crossed his fingers that nobody in the room knew he wasn't married any longer.

'So tell us about this person, Inspector.'

'He's of Algerian extraction, on the run in France for a couple of Post Office robberies, but not wanted in the UK for anything until he killed Nicholls.'

'And why did he do that?' asked an Army officer on his right. Gray thought for a moment. He thought that was the first time he had ever heard the Pongo speak. 'Have no idea sir. Hopefully we'll get to answer that when we catch him.'

'Was she attractive, the journalist?' asked the Flyboy sitting next to him.

'From what I understand, yes,' Gray replied.

'Well there's your answer then,' he continued, '*Cherchez la femme,* I always say. *Cherchez la femme.*' Gray was beginning to understand. The Military were in the room simply to provide a bit of colourful contrast to the drab grey suits on the left hand side of the table. And, as he thought about it, to waste a little time while the big burly Sergeant worked his magic on the phone.

'Any idea where he is at the moment Inspector?'

'We're narrowing it down a bit,' he replied. 'You know I can't go into any details at the moment.'

And then it happened. The Attorney General stood up, holding a phone, and said, 'I'm terribly sorry, I really do have to answer this.' She stood up holding the phone and started walking behind the chairs towards the double doors at the back of the room, where Gray had also stood up and intercepted her.

'I'll take that Mrs. MacStones,' he said taking the phone out of her hand, which was unprepared to resist such a sudden action, and released the phone without a struggle. Gray pressed the button on MacStones's phone, and said into it, "You can come in now Sergeant.'

'What do you mean by that?' spluttered the Attorney General.

'Katherine MacStones, you are under arrest for conspiring to assassinate the Prime Minister of the United Kingdom. You do not have to say anything, but anything you do say may be taken down and used in evidence.'

The huge grinning sergeant said, 'This way ma'am,' grabbing her by the upper arm while the Inspector behind him, produced a pair of handcuffs. Whether she actually said anything coherent to be taken down and used in evidence, Gray couldn't be sure.

There was a moment's silence while Gray resumed his seat.

Finally it was the Police Commissioner who broke the silence. 'How long have you known it was her?' she asked.

'For the last two minutes,' Gray replied. 'All I knew was that there was someone in this room who was leaking everything we have been saying back to the assassin. May I say how relieved I am that it was none of you still here present.' He went on to explain how the sting had worked, and added, 'I challenge anybody here to ignore a phone ringing continuously when you know the person on the other end is your assassin in the field who really, really wants to talk to you.'

'So where do we go from here?' asked the Home Secretary.

'Well the Assassin is really on his own now, so we wait for him to make a mistake.'

§§§§

Gray felt a lightness in his step as he got out of the car back at the flat. He replied cheerily, 'of course,' when Polly's voice asked him from the kitchen if he wanted coffee. Moments later she wandered in coffee in one hand and a mobile phone in her other, announcing, 'Your French policeman mate called about fifteen minutes ago, and asked if you would call him when you got back.'

'Why didn't you put him straight through?' Gray asked.

'Well we both knew you were in the middle of your takedown in the Home Office, and neither of us wanted to interfere with that. I like your French mate,' she added with a grin.

Had she been flirting with Truchaud, he wondered?

He tried to picture the slightly dishevelled middle-aged Frenchman with the metal faced Goth on his arm and the picture wouldn't focus, even if he reprocessed Polly in a daughter role. He picked up the phone and pressed the auto dial.

'How did it go?' Truchaud asked as soon as the call connected.

'The Spy is in custody,' Gray replied smugly.

'And who was it?'

'MacStones, the Attorney General.'

There was a pause from the other end and then Truchaud said, 'Well there's a facer. The person in charge of all the criminal activity in the country is herself guilty of planning to assassinate the prime minister. Is she guilty of treason? Do you still have a death penalty for treason? Who will decide, the Attorney General?'

'It's a plot line straight out of the Mikado,' said Gray.

'*Quoi?*'

'It was a musical comedy from the late nineteenth century. The Japanese were so fed up with the Executioner executing people for trivial offences that they elected the next person on the execution waiting list to be the new Lord High Executioner. He therefore was unable to decapitate anybody until he had cut his own head off.'

'And that was Victorian English humour?' asked Truchaud drily.

'Well it had some great tunes in it too,' said Gray back pedalling furiously. 'Anyway, Polly said you had something you wanted to tell me.'

'Oh yes, we arrested Mehdi Arraq fifteen kilometres out of Calais in the back of a truck heading south on the A26. I was slightly miffed, I had understood that if you were going to send him across the channel in a crate you would tip me the wink so we could arrest him. We only found him because he was in a truck, which we were already looking for being driven by a known felon. I have to say your people did a fairly good job on him, he wasn't immediately recognisable.'

Gray was completely nonplussed. 'What?' he said, 'I didn't know anything about it.'

'Well perhaps your Thames Valley Police did him over then.'

Gray didn't think that was very likely. If the Thames Valley Police had arrested him, he would be in a jail somewhere undergoing interrogation with a view to be being put on trial for the murder of Sierra Nicholls. He couldn't Imagine Becky or indeed anybody in Thames Valley simply whaling on him and then packing him up in a crate and sending him to France. In fact he was finding it quite difficult to imagine Becky at all, without it being a picture of her smiling amiably with her freckled nose slightly scrunched up, and those dimples in her cheeks. He came back to the now in a hurry. 'It is definitely him?' he asked.

'Oh yes definitely Mehdi. He has no idea what happened to him, but he has been talking in custody. He's in a Paris hospital.'

'Well I suppose that's that then,' said Gray after a moment feeling strangely deflated. Somehow the man he had been hunting for had ended up severely assaulted by person or persons unknown in a foreign country. 'I'll let the Met and the Thames Valley Police know you've got him.'

'Okay my friend,' replied Truchaud, 'No doubt we will talk again soon. Try to get over here sometime and we'll have a drink. I cracked open a bottle of our 2010 Vosne the other day for the first time.'

'Oh, how was it?'

'Superb! We all knew there was going to be something special about the 2010 Bourgogne if you left them long enough. We were right. *À bientôt*,' and the phone disconnected.

Gray looked across at Watts and Polly who were looking at him with puzzled expressions on their faces. 'The French have got him,' he said. 'I need to contact the Met and Thames Valley to let them know.

'Hello Auntie Muriel,' he said into his phone, while Polly and Watts listened with considerable interest. 'It appears the French have got Smilodon.' There was a pause and then he continued, 'No I don't think they're going to let us have access to him any time soon.' A further pause followed and then he said, 'Firstly he was pretty badly beaten up and he's in hospital, and secondly he's got some very seriously serious charges to answer on their side of the channel at the moment. Incidentally, do we still have an extradition treaty with the French? I know that was spaffed up the wall with some of our European 'Friends and Allies' as soon as Brexit was enacted.' He paused again while a slightly embarrassed flush spread up his features, finally he replied, 'Sorry, guv but you did ask.' And he disconnected the phone.

He then picked up his own regular phone and when it was answered he asked to be put through to DI Sharp. 'Hi Becky,' he said, 'Gray here.' He then repeated the story to her too. From his expression Polly and Watts could tell that she too was more than a little disappointed. He then put the phone down on the table.

'So that's it for us,' said Polly glumly. 'You know, I'm rather sad about that, I've rather enjoyed working with you two.' She then brightened up, 'Still it's not all bad news, I'll get to see my boyfriend later, so it's nookie for me tonight.'

'I'm sure we'll meet up again,' he replied wondering whenever that might happen. It wasn't as if he moved in circles that featured cockney Goths in Hemel Hempstead.

They started assembling the various bits of kit that would need to be returned to their rightful owners. The various phones would need to go back to the Met, where they would be suitably cleaned.

'May as well finish the milk,' said Polly, 'Fancy another coffee guys?'

'Why not,' said Watts, who was disassembling a pistol and removing the bullets from it.

'I didn't know you had one of those,' Polly said. 'Are you any good with it?'

'We'll never know with this one,' he replied, 'but generally speaking I'm not a bad shot.'

The coffee mugs were on the table and steaming. Each of them was shutting down what each of them was shutting down, rather sadly. Neither of them was quite sure who first became aware of the phone vibrating on the table. What was certain was that they were all looking at each other when they were aware of it.

'Pass it here,' said Gray.

He pressed the answer button on it. It was a text which read, 'Where the fuck are you? I keep calling and calling you, you silly bitch and you don't call back. Call back immediately do you hear?'

'Which phone is this?' Gray asked.

'It was the clone of the Spy's phone,' Polly said, 'Look, you can tell by the flash of nail varnish on the side.'

'You used nail varnish on a phone?'

'Well I wasn't going to use that disgusting pink colour on anything else now was I?'

'So that was Smilodon texting MacStones?' said Gray slowly as the truth began to impact on all three of them. 'So it wasn't Smilodon who was beaten up and shipped off to France after all.'

'It appears not,' said Watts. 'Oh shit! I don't know whether to laugh or cry.'

'Well, it appears we're not disbanded yet anyway,' said Polly sounding a lot happier.

'Have either of you heard from Inspector Anson over his Stuart Ingram bloke? He seems to have gone very quiet over the last twenty-four hours.'

'If I'd heard anything I'd have told you, guv,' said Watts while Polly started rummaging round the various phones on the table to see whether a message had come through while she wasn't looking.

'Nuffink here, guv,' she said once she had checked all the phones.

Gray took out his phone and called Auntie Muriel again. 'What can I do for you Chief Inspector?' she asked politely.

'We appear to have hit a glitch,' he said.

'I've got a feeling I'm not going to like this,' she said. The acidity in her tone was detectable even down a cellular phone.

'It appears that the man arrested by the French was not Smilodon.'

'And you know this how?' and Gray explained what had happened. After the Commissioner had calmed down she asked him what he thought they ought to do next, and he asked if she had heard anything about Anson's investigation.

'Nothing recently,' she replied, 'nothing since they searched Ingram's place and started looking for fake passports, no. Do you want to call him directly? I'll send you his number.'

Five minutes later Gray had got through to Inspector Anson's number, and he was asking how his investigation was going.'

'Well, we've found him,' Anson replied.

'That doesn't sound very positive,' said Gray, 'You don't sound excited.'

'I'm not. He's a very nasty little toe rag, but he's not your man.'

'Go on.' Gray felt hollow in the pit of his stomach, but he still wanted to know the whole story.

'Well Ingram did indeed set up a fake passport, but that's because Stuart Ingram is no longer allowed to enter South Africa. Therefore if he turned up at Johannesburg Airport on his own passport, they would put him back on the plane and send it on to God knows where.'

'May I ask why?'

'He's a big game trafficker. So in order to do what he planned to do, he needed to be somebody else. Once into South Africa, he knew where to go to get a high powered rifle and a band saw. He went into one of the game reserves and shot a couple of rhinos. With his band saws he cut off the horns and put them into a bag. Quite how he got from South Africa to Vietnam isn't clear at the moment, but he then sold the horns in a black market in Hanoi. They're apparently very into the, shall we say, erectile effect of Rhino horn in

Vietnam.'

'But that's a load of bollocks!' Gray exclaimed.

'You know that, and I know that, and for that matter Ingram knows that too, but the Vietnamese apparently don't and Ingram is very happy about separating fools from their money.'

'At the expense of the life of a rare and protected species?'

'You've got it in one.'

'So what are you going to do?'

'Don't know yet, but the team is thinking about offering to extradite him to South Africa if they want him.'

'And what will they do to him?'

'Whatever they damn well want! However mate, I'm afraid that doesn't solve your problem at all does it?'

'I'm afraid not. Okay, well, stay in touch,' and Gray disconnected. He knew he was going to have another very difficult conversation with the Commissioner.

The bottom line of his conversation with the Commissioner was that he'd better come back to the Home Office to brief the Home Secretary, to advise the Prime Minister that he would be wise to go into hiding for the time being.

§§§§

Gray looked across at Watts. The driver's face was expressionless, but then he wasn't going to have to tell the Home Secretary, face to face, that he had failed, and that he had no idea who Smilodon is. He'd been quite convinced he'd been Truchaud's man, the man who had killed the reporter. Admittedly all the evidence had been circumstantial, but it had all continued to move in the same direction. Now he knew that was not the case. Gray was driving the big engined car at a respectful speed, so that they didn't arrive at the Home Office at any time before they should.

'What's that?' Watts asked pointing forward through the windscreen into the road ahead.

'What?' asked Gray trying to work out what Watts was talking about.

'About eight feet up, there's two of them.'

Oh yes. There were a pair of cheap and cheerful drones such as you could buy from any electronics stores pottering forwards. There was one major difference between them and your average drone; they were travelling at roughly the same speed as the car the two of them were travelling in.

'Follow them,' said Gray almost stentorially.

'I was going to,' Watts replied. 'Do you want blues and twos?'

Gray thought about it for a moment. 'Only if we run into traffic and start to lose them.' After all that part of London wasn't that busy on Sunday afternoon. They both looked thoughtfully down the turn off from Birdcage Walk that they would have taken to get to the Home Office. The drones flew up Great George Street, with the souped up Vectra in pursuit. At the statue of Sir Winston Churchill, the drones turned sharp left, as if they were repelled by it as much as the great man himself was reputed to have been.

'You know where they're going, don't you guv?' said Watts, still following the drones.

'I've got a very shrewd idea,' he replied. He leant over the back of his seat and felt for the rifle that was hidden under the passenger seat. In the glove compartment in front of him, he found the box of live rounds, and started loading the rifle. When the drones hopped over the gates into Downing Street, the rifle was loaded and ready. They hadn't got time to call for clearance to open the gates to let them in. When they were opposite Downing Street, he said loudly. 'Stop!' and leapt out of the car pulling the rifle up to his shoulder. He took aim at the nearest of the drones, squeezed the trigger, and missed. He knew he had missed, because a first floor window of Number Ten shattered.

A voice from Downing Street shouted, 'Down on the road now. Drop the gun…' He didn't have time to complete the sentence as Watts who had raced round the front of the car and was now crouched next to Gray, said, 'Here; give it to me.' He took the rifle out of Gray's hand aimed and fired at the drone. There was an enormous flash of white light, like a magnesium flare followed by a noise like a thunderclap.

There was a moment of silence and Watts muttered, 'Five years in the Marines,' followed by a bullet whistling between their heads and crashing through the passenger window of the Vectra. 'The next bullet will hit one of you,' said the voice from Downing Street. 'Down on the ground, now.'

Gray and Watts looked each other in the eye and followed the command. Watts laid the rifle gently in the street. They watched the surviving drone rise over the roofline of Number 10 and disappear out of sight.

The armed police had reached the gates and were just entering Downing Street when a second brilliant white flash appeared over the roof line and an if anything even bigger explosion reached their ears.

'What the fuck have you two lunatics done?'

shouted the soldier running towards them putting another bullet into the car behind them.

'What the fuck did the poor car do to deserve being shot up,' retorted Watts putting both hands on top of his head.

A thought passed through his mind as Gray felt the handcuffs being applied, which he voiced to everybody's puzzlement, 'A hundred and five per cent.'

THE NOVELLA NOSTALGIA SERIES

This publishing initiative brings together the uniqueness of the novella and various memorable movies from the history of cinema.

The word 'novella' comes from the Italian for 'novel.' It has been interpreted in various ways including 'a long short story' or a 'short novel'. It can be traced back to the early renaissance in Italy and France. Giovanni Boccaccio wrote 'The Decameron' in 1353. This comprises 100 tales of ten people fleeing the black death. It was not until the 18th and 19th centuries that the novella emerged as a literary genre.

In 1941, the Austrian novelist Stefan Zweig wrote 'The Chess Novella' which was later renamed 'The Royal Game'. This was the inspiration for the 1960 film 'Brainwashed'.

Most modern novellas are published by Penguin Modern Classics. The various novella prizes seem to stipulate a word count of between 7,500 and 40,000. A key feature of the novella is its limited punctuation. There are no chapter headings and no breaks apart from spaces where the author needs to show a scene change.

Full details of the Novella Nostalgia series can be found at www.cityfiction.co.uk.

ABOUT THE AUTHOR

Richard (Dick) Cartmel is a retired General Practitioner and lives in Peterborough, United Kingdom.

He has combined his love of fine wines, politics and human nature when writing a series of six novels.

A French police officer features in three - *The Inspector Truchaud Mystery* series - which takes him into the vineyards of Burgundy.

His well-reviewed book, *North Sea Rising*, envisages a post-Brexit Britain in 2039.

Dick Cartmel cleverly picks up this theme in his novella *The White House: Holyhead*. This is his first publication for City Fiction Limited.

Full details and contact can be found on:

Email   dick.cartmel@gmail.com
WWW   rmcartmelauthor.com
Twitter   @cartmelDr

Printed in Great Britain
by Amazon